GULL!

by

John Birkett

Published in 2008 by YouWriteOn.com

First Edition

Published by YouWriteOn.com

Gull!

Chapter 1

Rocks

There are so many things to look for when you walk on a beach: sea creatures, interesting shells and pebbles, messages in bottles washed in with the tide and really anything your imagination can come up with. But in looking down or out to sea you don't often look behind you and upwards. And that can be a big mistake!

For some people it might be a gull that rudely awakens them from their daydreams, coating their heads with a stinking, slimy white reminder of where they are. For twelve year old Aimee it was something much less embarrassing and far more frightening...

The morning's storm had turned to a light drizzle and as she stooped to pick up an interesting little pink, gold and white shell the first crumbs of clay began to fall into her hair and over her back. Before she had the chance to look up, the crumbs turned to clods and within seconds a whole mass of clay, soil and small stones had slumped down on top of her. She didn't have much time to scream and then she couldn't as her mouth filled with mud. She was sent sprawling to the sand by the overwhelming mass of debris until only the top left half of her head remained uncovered and she was just about able breathe through one nostril.

After several minutes the realisation of what had happened pushed its way through the fog of shock. "I've got to shout for help... the tide will be starting to come in soon."

She wiggled her fingers but it soon became obvious that her right arm was trapped underneath her body and her left, though to the side, was held fast by the clay and stones. She tried pushing the mud out of her mouth with her tongue but although she managed to empty it, it was still below the soil and the weight pressing down on her back meant that breathing was so difficult that anything more than a squeak was near to impossible.

"Oh please, someone come, please," she thought and again she tried to move her left hand. Her fingers managed a little wriggle and moved a few fragments of earth while the rest of her hand and arm was locked solidly in place. Another wriggle loosened a little more earth, but it was obvious that unless help came soon she was going to be at the mercy of the sea. "Help, oh please, someone, help."

Then more thoughts started to come to her, thoughts of her mum, her brother, Jamie and her dad... her dad, five years gone now. She might never see Mum and Jamie again...but she might see Dad... No, she had to keep trying to move, to shout, and to dig.

She again tried to wriggle, to claw at the earth and slowly she managed to move enough of it to begin to turn her whole hand a little, but enough to give hope.

"Yes," she thought, "I can do it, I will do it, I will escape!"

She wriggled and clawed and moved until more and more movement came to her left hand and then a little to her arm as she was able to push it forward into the space her hand had made. They were just little bits of movement but they seemed to Aimee like great leaps.

With her limited hearing she tried to listen for any noises that might mean people were around, footsteps in the sand, children shouting, or dogs barking – that would be great, they'd be bound to sniff her out! But all she could hear was the sound of waves getting closer. And then another sound came to her, one she didn't recognise at first because she'd never heard one so close up before. A gull had landed so very close by that she felt the draught from its wings on the top of her head.

The gull walked in circles around Aimee's head, investigating what the landslip had brought… and then to her horror it began to peck.

Aimee screamed in her mind but could get no more than a whimper out of her mouth. Her left hand grasped and scraped more and more frantically, getting extra movement to her arm, but not enough to help. Pain seared through her head as the gull's sharp beak tore into her scalp and pulled at her mud soaked, brown hair.

Her fingers again pushed forward into the earth, given more power now by the pain and fear the gull had created. Then they touched something that blocked their way, something smooth…and warm. She scratched around its outline, trying to get a hold on it to pull it away while the gull again pecked and this time tore open a small flap of flesh on Aimee's head. The pain made her shake as she managed to whimper a stifled, "I want to go home!" before her mind gave up and she lost consciousness.

Chapter 2

Hospital

As her mind slowly drifted back Aimee became aware of the sound of footsteps on a hard floor… and then voices… and then a strong smell of antiseptic… and then light, lots of light. She forced open her eyes and found two browny-green eyes staring at her, the nose beneath them almost touching hers. She could feel the warm breath coming from it and then the nose moved and a mouth took its place. The mouth opened and Aimee caught a strong whiff of orange chews before it gave out a very loud and excited squeal.

"Mum, Mum…she's back, she's awake, Aimee's awake!"

"Aimee, oh Aimee, love!" gushed her mother as she spun round from her conversation with a man in a black suit, "How are you feeling? Are you alright?"

Aimee looked up at her and then at her younger brother, Jamie. She gathered her thoughts as best she could through the fog of waking and the throb of her aching head. "Where am I? My head hurts," was all she could manage but just hearing her voice seemed to have an instant effect on her Mum and she burst into tears.

"You're in hospital, love," Mum managed between sobs, "And your head will hurt; you've… you've got a right nasty cut on it."

Jamie couldn't contain himself, "Yeah, it's a real good rip, a flap this big," he held out his hand and flapped it up and down, "Big enough for your brains to fall out, if you had any that is." He smiled at his own joke and then his face turned serious," I bet you did it to try and get off school next week!" and he really seemed to mean it. Mum looked daggers at him.

8

"Did what? What did I do? Why am I in hospital?" Aimee asked, her face frowning with confusion, tiredness and pain.

A sturdy looking nurse with greying ginger hair came briskly down the ward and interrupted, "Ah, Aimee, you've woken up I see. You've had us all worried you know. How are you feeling, are you thirsty, do you want anything to eat?"

Aimee leant forward and was sick down the front of Jamie's best denims.

"I take it that means no!" the nurse said quite matter of factly.

"Oh thanks, Sis, I love you too!" Jamie blurted and ran down the ward to the toilet to be sick himself.

"Sorry," she managed to say, "It just came out, I couldn't help it… sorry."

"Don't worry about it; it happens a lot in here. Now, besides a cloth and bucket, is there anything I can get for you?" asked the nurse.

"My head aches and I would like a drink please…Is that your real name, Dina Sawyer?" smiled Aimee as she read the name badge on the nurse's uniform.

"Yes it is and if you make any remarks about prehistoric creatures I'll let that brother of yours stay in the next bed like he's been wanting to," she replied, "I'll get you some painkillers and water – we'll have another go at the food later." She wiped up what sick had made it past Jamie to the floor and went to check on him.

"Er…Mum, who is that man in the tatty black suit; he's not an undertaker is he? Did you think I was…?"

By now Mrs Hawthorne had stopped crying, wiped her eyes and was busily applying a new layer of lipstick. "Oh no dear, of course not," she smiled both at Aimee and at her mirror, "He's from the police."

"The police! Why? What have I done? What happened to me? Ohhh, my head aches."

"Here we are, Aimee, swallow this and it will take the pain away," the Dinasawyer had returned followed by a rather pale looking Jamie. "Are you going to stand around there all day?" she had now turned her attention to the policeman. "You're making the ward look untidy," she said and strode away to attend to another patient further down the ward.

The policeman looked startled as if he had been woken from a deep daydream, which in fact he had. "Oh... Er... I was just, er, waiting to see if Aimee was ready to answer a few questions yet... Er... I'm sorry if I'm in the way, I'll move if you like."

"Why don't you sit down here out of the way?" Mrs Hawthorne smiled looking up at the policeman and she patted the seat where Jamie had been sitting. Before he could reply Jamie neatly side-stepped the policeman and plonked himself down next to his mum. She again gave him a hard stare and moved across to sit on the edge of the bed, pointed to the chair and looked at the policeman saying, "There we are, plenty of room for all of us.

"Thank you, Mrs Hawthorne, I'm Detective Constable Martin and I really do need to talk to Aimee if she's ready, we need to try and clear up this little mystery."

"Mystery, what mystery?" Aimee asked, "What happened to me, why am I here?"

"Well, Aimee, I'm hoping that you will be able to help us to work out what happened to you, but as for why you are here that's easy. Your brother found you collapsed on your doorstep last night when he got back from football training."

"Yeah, you were in a right mess, covered with muck and loads of blood on your head," Jamie told his part of the story excitedly, "So I shouted for Mum and rang for the emergency services; I probably saved your life!

"And I bet you won't let me forget it," Aimee smiled.

"Yes," said Mum, "The police arrived first, then the ambulance and then the FIRE BRIGADE!"

"I like fire engines," Jamie explained as if that was a good excuse for wasting their time.

"So you can see we need to try and work out how you got into that state and whether anyone else was involved," interrupted D.C. Martin. "Can you remember anything at all about what happened to you Aimee?"

Mrs Hawthorne gently squeezed Aimee's hand, "Try and remember, love."

Aimee frowned and thought hard. She could remember having eggs on toast for breakfast and Jamie getting in a right strop because Mum wouldn't give him any pocket money before she went to work because he hadn't mowed the lawn yet, even though he had promised faithfully that he would two weeks ago. She remembered foolishly letting him have enough money to go to football training knowing that it would be the last she saw of the 'loan.' And the last thing that she could remember was setting out for a walk after making the two of them some banana butties for lunch, which Jamie ate as he set off for the sports centre. That was it; walking on the beach was the last thing that came to mind. She told all this to D.C. Martin and he wrote it down in his notebook and sighed. There wasn't much to go on there.

He stood up and reached into the inside pocket of his suit jacket. "Right, if that is all you can think of I'll be getting back to the station to see if they've worked out where the mud was from. If anything else comes back to you just give me a ring on this number," and he gave the card to Aimee's mum for safe keeping. With that he gave Aimee a smile and he and Mum walked down the ward for a quick word with Nurse Sawyer before he left.

Jamie looked at his sister suspiciously. "So come on then, what did happen?"

"Honestly, Jamie, I really can't remember. I was walking on the beach and then I was here!"

"And what about all the muck, the hole in the head and the bottle?" persisted Jamie.

"What bottle, what are you going on about?" She was beginning to get rattled by her brother and her inability to remember anything.

Jamie smiled, "It's at home. You were really holding on to it – I had to prise your fingers off it! I've hidden it… it looks old and I didn't want the cops to take it. It might be worth something!"

"What does it look like?" Aimee asked, puzzled about why she'd had a bottle in her hand.

"Oh, it's sort of old looking, about the size of my fist and it's got some green oily looking stuff inside. It's got a square body and a round neck with like a marble stuck in it for a stopper," Jamie smiled, "And you'll never guess where I hid it!"

"I will, Jamie, because you owe me five pounds and Mum doesn't know about me lending it to you and she doesn't know about the Capo de Monte figure that you cracked when you were playing soldiers with it."

Jamie scowled, "I'll keep it safe for you… but you have to have a go at finding it cos' it's in a great hiding place."

Nurse Sawyer and Mrs Hawthorn came back down the ward deep in conversation. As they reached the bed they both turned to look at Aimee and Mum said, "Nurse Sawyer here tells me that you can come home tomorrow. They want to keep you in another night to make sure you're alright."

The nurse added, "We'll make sure your cut is beginning to heal properly, change the dressings and keep you under observation just in case you're still a bit dizzy."

"How will you tell, she's always a bit dizzy!" Jamie quipped.

"Would you like to ask the nurse if she's got a cure for your earache while we're here dear?" asked Mum.

"But I haven't got earache, Mum." Jamie replied looking puzzled. Aimee smirked as she guessed what was coming. Mum leant across to Jamie and got hold of him by his right ear, pulling him to his feet and down the ward towards the exit with it.

"I said would you like to ask the nurse if she's got a cure for earache!" she smiled as she turned and called, "See you tomorrow, love. Bye' nurse, look after her, besides this thing she's all I've got!"

"Goodbye, Mrs Hawthorn, don't worry she'll be ready for you tomorrow, bright-eyed and bushy-tailed."

"Watch out, Sis' the dinosaur's going to turn you into a squirrel!" Jamie shouted as they left the ward, then, "Ooow!"

"Now, we'll have a little look at your cut, put a fresh dressing on it and then I want you to try and get as much rest as you can. You've had a bad experience, whatever it was," Nurse Dina said softly as she unwrapped Aimee's head. "Mmm… That seems to be nice and clean, the stitches are very neat, you shouldn't have much of a scar and even that should be hidden under your hair. No 'Harry Potter' zigzag for you, Aimee Hawthorn!" and she grinned as she put the new dressing on, "Try and rest and I'll be along to check on you a little later."

Aimee thought for a while about the bottle, she seemed to have something in the dark caves of her mind about touching something smooth and hard… like glass. Maybe that was the bottle. Maybe she was holding the bottle when… when what? And with that question in her mind she drifted off to sleep.

"Aimee, Aimee, it's time to wake up now. What would you like for breakfast?" the voice was soft and close by her ear. Aimee opened her eyes with a struggle and tried to focus on the face that was speaking to her. It wasn't Nurse Dina but the face looked kind and unthreatening so she decided it was alright to reply.

"Hello… you're not Nurse Dina"

The new nurse smiled and said in her quiet low voice, "My, aren't you the clever one to spot that. I'm nurse Alycia Williams, Dina went off duty after you went to sleep last night. She'll be back later though, in time to see you off home - if the Doctor says you can go that is."

She turned to walk away then stopped and turned back again. "By the way, did you sleep alright only you were making some pretty strange noises at times and you were shouting out as well?"

Aimee thought hard but she couldn't remember any dreams. "What was I shouting?"

Nurse Alycia looked down at her watch. "Good, I'm off duty in ten minutes. Er, I think it was something like…girl or gill or gull. It was hard to make out because you were really screeching it. I had to shake you to stop you waking the rest of the hospital up!" she smiled, "I didn't wake you though, proper gone you were!"

"Girl, gill, gull"…something was there in those mind caves again, but what was it? "A bottle, girl, gill, gull…gull…Yes, gull, that's what hits the button…But why?" Aimee closed her eyes tight, trying to reach deep into her mind to grasp the memory that she knew was there…somewhere.

"Do you want any juice with your breakfast, Aimee? Its porridge today- the breakfast I mean, not the juice- that's orange." Nurse

Alycia asked.

"Yes please, I'm starving!" answered Aimee; suddenly realising her belly was rumbling away to itself.

"Right, I'll tell the catering ladies. I'm off now…Bye!"

"What time will the doctor be coming?" Aimee called after her.

"Oh, about eleven o'clock," She called back as she disappeared around the end of the ward.

Breakfast arrived a little later. The juice looked pale and thin and the porridge looked grey and thick but both tasted wonderful and having washed it down with equally grey looking but refreshing tea Aimee asked the new nurse, Nurse Mandy, if she could go to the toilet.

"Of course you can, but I'd better walk with you to make sure you're steady enough on your feet. You were a right mess when we got you yesterday you know. I'm pleased you're looking a lot brighter now. How do you feel?" Nurse Mandy replied with a broad smile spread across her broad face.

"Not too bad thanks," Aimee smiled back, "I just wish I knew what happened to me."

As they walked along the ward to the toilet Nurse Mandy introduced her to the other invalids. Most looked very pale and managed only a small smile in return to their greeting but one small, frail looking girl sat up and cheerfully called out, "Hello, I'm Belinda, I'm six and this is my doggy." She held up a threadbare stuffed puppy with ears that were wet and shrinking with being chewed. "He's called, Puppy Dog. Say hello, Puppy Dog," and she waved one of his paws at Aimee who smiled and waved back. "Did Doctor Gill help you to sleep last night? He spent a long time talking to you."

Nurse Mandy looked puzzled, "We haven't got a, Doctor Gill at this hospital as far as I know, Belinda."

15

"Oh but he came last night to see Aimee! I was awake and he told me to go to sleep, but I didn't. I read his badge. It said, "Doctor C. Gill" and I tried to listen to what he was saying to you because you looked horrible when you came in yesterday and I was worried about you and I think you're very nice." Belinda spoke quickly but in a tone that sounded very sincere.

"I saw him as well, he was very tall!" The voice was frail and belonged to Cyanne in the next bed to Belinda.

Nurse Mandy looked worried and said, "I'm just going to find out who this Doctor Gill is, I've never heard of him… and what was he doing in the ward in the middle of the night? Alycia didn't say anything about him when she passed her notes on. Can you manage the toilet on your own?"

Aimee nodded, she had another piece to put into the jigsaw, Doctor Gill…girl, gull…

When she returned from the toilet she found Nurse Mandy stood by her bed looking at her notes with another nurse, both were frowning and talking in hushed but obviously worried tones.

"What is it?" Aimee asked, "Have you found out about Doctor Gill, I don't remember seeing him. Did he really come?"

Both nurses turned to her and though they were trying to appear calm and unworried she could tell from their eyes that this, Doctor Gill was worrying them greatly. It was the new nurse who spoke first, her eyes fixed on Aimee's and her face trying to convey calmness, "Now, Aimee, there really is nothing to worry about but…"

"…But what? Who is, Doctor Gill? Was he here last night or wasn't he? I didn't talk to him! I didn't even see him!" Aimee tried to keep calm but there was too much she didn't know and it was becoming too much for her to handle, "What is happening!" she shrieked as a cloudburst of tears flooded her cheeks.

16

She sat down heavily on her bed and wiped her eyes and her equally flooded nose on a tissue that Nurse Mandy gave to her. The new nurse gave Nurse Mandy a glance and flick of her head and she turned and pulled the screens around the bed then went to 'see' to the others on the ward.

The new nurse sat down on the bed next to Aimee and spoke with a quiet, serious voice, "l am the ward sister and we haven't met yet because you were asleep when I came on duty today. My name is Charlotte and I'm going to be honest with you, Aimee. According to Belinda and Cyanne you were visited by a Doctor Gill last night. They both say they saw him and they both gave the same description of him. They say he talked to you for quite a while before he went."

Aimee began to cry again making it difficult for her to reply, "But I didn't see him or talk to him… honestly!" she managed.

"I believe you, Aimee," Sister Charlotte reassured her, "But you see I've worked here for a long time and I don't know of any Doctor Gill. I've even checked with the local health authority and they haven't heard of him either.

"So you think Belinda and Cyanne are li…telling tales." Aimee decided to be careful in her choice of words. She was beginning to calm down now that she saw that the nurses were as worried as she was. And besides, she liked a good mystery - she just didn't like being at the centre of it very much, especially as her memory of events had such great gaps in it.

"I suppose so… but they do seem so certain of what they saw and they seem to be nice honest children. Anyway, why should they make up a story like that? I think we'll have to presume they dreamt it all… but it is very puzzling. Try not to let it get to you though; you just concentrate on getting yourself better. Now let's have a look at that cut of yours."

Aimee sat and had her dressing changed by the gentle hands of the ward sister but all the time her mind was roving back and forth over the events of the last 24 hours.

"Good, that is looking nice. I think the doctor will let you go home this afternoon."

The mention of the Doctor jumped Aimee back into the present again. She looked shocked as she asked, "What Doctor?"

Sister Charlotte smiled, "I'm sorry, I didn't mean to upset you. It's the duty doctor, Doctor Dhutta. She stitched you up yesterday, and a good job she made of it I would say. She just needs to check you out before we let you go home but I think you'll be alright, Aimee. You seem to be a tough un'." And she smiled again as she turned to pull back the screens.

Aimee smiled back, home would be nice. She could upset Jamie by finding the bottle and maybe that would help to fill in some of the blanks. "Now where would he have hidden it? Where does he think he can put it that I don't know about?" Aimee muttered to herself. "Not in the lavatory cistern, he used that for my watch, the rat! Not in the loft, he's still afraid of the 'boggle' that lives there... Ah...got it!"

Chapter 3

Bottle

After Doctor Dhutta had told her not to overdo things for a few days and not to do whatever she had done again, she was allowed to leave.

While her mum was talking to the nurses, Belinda and Cyanne beckoned to Aimee to come over. As she approached, Belinda put her finger to her lips, looked around and satisfied that no one would overhear she quietly but firmly said, "I wasn't fibbing you know. Doctor Gill did come and he did talk to you. And I didn't dream it either. He was asking you questions but you didn't talk very much and when you started shouting he went away. I don't think he was very happy with you, he had an angry look on his face."

"I didn't like him!" whispered Cyanne, "I didn't get back to sleep after he'd been."

Mrs Hawthorn turned from the nurses and called to Aimee to come. "I've got a taxi booked to take us home so hurry up, Aimee."

Aimee said her goodbyes to the other girls, thanked the nurses and they left.

"Where to ladies?" The taxi driver asked as he turned the ignition key.

"18 Lawton Crescent please," Mrs Hawthorn replied as she helped Aimee with her seat belt and hugging her close as the taxi pulled away. "He's rather sweet isn't he, Aimee?"

But Aimee had her attention elsewhere. There, sitting on the gate posts at the end of the drive, was a large gull. She looked intently at it and as the taxi drove past the gull looked down at her and gave a loud and raucous cry that sounded like a laugh. It was a laugh that sent a chilling shiver right through Aimee, and at that same moment the words she had screamed in the night came back to her, "Girl, gill, GULL!"

Mum nudged her back to the taxi.

"Eh… er…yes, Mum...er…who is?"

"Dave, the driver…he's nice isn't he?"

"Mum!"

They continued the journey in silence; Aimee watching for another sighting of the gull and Mum holding her hand and staring at her. As they neared home Mum made her jump again as she suddenly turned her attentions back to Dave.

"How long have you been a taxi driver then, Dave?"

Dave glanced over his shoulder and replied, "About three years, ever since I left the ice cream factory."

"Oh yes, and why did you leave then, Dave?" Mum asked, expecting to hear some interesting tale of standing up to bullying managers or having his ideas for a new and better way of making ice cream stolen and used by them. She waited, ready to sympathise and offer her services as a good listener, perhaps over a meal one night.

The taxi had just arrived outside number 18 as Dave turned to answer, "I got the sack for sneezing into the triple mint and choc whipple mixer," he explained as he wiped his nose on the back of his sleeve.

Mrs Hawthorn paid him quickly and hurried to open the door

without a backward glance. Aimee doubled up in the back of the taxi gurgling with laughter.

"Works every time," Dave said proudly with a huge smile across his face, "My wife would kill me if I let myself be chatted up. Trouble is I don't get as many tips!" He helped Aimee out of the taxi and wished her a speedy recovery before he drove off down the road.

Aimee watched the taxi to the end of the road and then turned to go to the house. There, sat on the top of the roof was a gull, the gull – she had no doubts about that.

It stared down at her.

She stared up at it. "Who are you?" she breathed and then was startled as the bird looked away from her towards the road and, giving its raucous laughing cry, spread its wings and took off. It circled in the air and then wheeled away over the field towards the cliff tops.

"Hiya, Sis'! They've let you out of the funny farm then. Welcome home, Scarface!" Jamie shouted. But she didn't turn, she just stood and stared, transfixed by the flight of the gull until it dipped out of view over the edge of the cliffs.

Putting his hand on her shoulder did the trick though and she wheeled around and screeched, "Jamie, don't you ever sneak up on me like that again!" She burst into tears and ran into the house, went straight up to her room and slammed the door shut behind her.

"Nice to see you too, Jamie," Jamie said to himself and shrugged his shoulders, went into the house and called out, "What's for tea, Mum, I'm starving!"

Mum was standing in the kitchen waiting for him.

"What have you said to upset her then? You know she's a bit delicate at the moment since... well since whatever happened. You really have got to try and be nice to her you know," she said sharply.

"But I only said "Welcome home," Mum…honestly!" Jamie replied, his feelings hurt. He actually liked his sister even if she was a girl. She wasn't one of those silly, 'look at my new clothes,' sisters that the other boys in his school seemed to have. She could play football pretty well and didn't mind if she got bruised. In fact she actually did most of the bruising! She was a good big sister to Jamie, though he wouldn't want to admit it to her. He had been genuinely upset when he'd found her on the doorstep. Not just because of the cut and the blood and the mud, but because he hated the thought that someone had done this to HIS sister. And now she was different and he couldn't understand why.

"Try to be nice to her, Jamie, just for a little while, love, till she's a bit stronger eh," Mum said more gently; she knew that he cared but he was a bit insensitive at times.

"I will, Mum, I promise." He looked into her eyes and could see that she was as worried as he was. "I'll go and say sorry to her and be all sympathetic like," he smiled.

Mum smiled back, "Do your best, that's a good lad."

Jamie ran up the stairs and knocked gently on Aimee's door. There was no reply so he knocked louder. Still no reply so he knocked as loud as he dare.

"If that's you, Dogbreath I don't want to see you!" she shouted.

"Aw, come on, Sis' I want to say I'm sorry. I didn't mean to upset you. I was really glad to see you were home. Open the door, come on, Aimee."

The door opened just a little and Aimee spoke through the gap, "If you're going to say you're sorry you must do it on your knees. You must grovel for my forgiveness." He couldn't see her smile.

"Grovel!" he sputtered, "You've got to be j..." then he remembered his promise to Mum and sank to the floor. "Alright, I'm down on my knees. Now open the door please."

The door opened slowly and Aimee's face appeared around the corner of it. She started to laugh, not only at Jamie who was knelt down with his nose to the carpet muttering "I'm sorry, I'm sorry," but because Mum was stood behind him holding her mouth trying not to burst out laughing as well.

Jamie looked up, saw Aimee, saw where she was looking, looked around, saw Mum and said quietly, "It had better be spaghetti Bolognese for tea!"

"It will be, love, it will be," said Mum as she went back down the stairs still giggling.

Aimee pulled Jamie into her room and pushed him onto the chair. "Sit down," she said when he was sat down. "I'm sorry I went off like that in the garden…it's just that… I've got something… er… something on my mind at the moment and you startled me."

"You startled me as well! I've never seen you like that before. What is it then? You're not worried about going back to school tomorrow are you?"

"School, oh no! I'm not going back tomorrow; I've not to go back for another two weeks. The Doctor said so," Aimee answered.

"Two weeks! Two weeks off school… you jammy grotbag! Two weeks for a little scratch on your head!" Jamie was astounded by her good luck, forgetting all about her ordeal.

"Look, Jamie, forget about school… I think I might need your help. I've got to try and sort out what happened to me. Something strange is going on and I don't know what or why it's happening to me.

"Two whole weeks…By the time you get back it will nearly be the summer holidays! You jammy grotbag!"

"Jamie!"

"Alright, I'll help you. But it'll cost you. You have to do my homework for me until the end of term. That way I'll have time to help you, won't I?"

"It's a deal. Now first you can go and fetch the bottle from the hole under the shed and we'll have a look at it to see if there are any clues," Aimee agreed.

"Right…Hey, how did you know I'd hidden it there?

Aimee smiled and waved him away adding as he got to the top stair, "You're my little brother, I know everything about you…and don't you forget it!"

He returned a few minutes later holding a green plastic bag in which he had wrapped the metal toolbox, in which he had put Freddy the hamster's old straw bedding, in which he had put the brown paper bag that now contained the bottle. He could be a careful boy when he wanted to be!

Aimee had just got to the brown paper bag when…"Aimee, Jamie…your spaghetti's ready. Come and get it!"

They put the bag back in the box and put the box under Jamie's bed before bounding down to eat - you don't keep Mum waiting when she's cooked you spaghetti Bolognese! They adored spaghetti Bolognese! Next to ice cream and chocolate and possibly fish and chips with mushy peas it was their favourite.

Jamie's jealousy over the two weeks off school did melt a little bit as he sucked the first strands of spaghetti into his mouth letting the rich beefy, tomato sauce collect and dribble around his lips before using his tongue to slurp them clean. It was a noisy and messy way of eating but essential to get the maximum pleasure out of spaghetti Bolognese – for Jamie anyway – it made Aimee and Mum feel sick!

His jealousy melted even more as he tucked in to ice cream smothered in chocolate sauce for afters. This was a real treat to welcome Aimee home, and he was loving it!

Aimee still had her thoughts on the bottle, she still hadn't seen it and, though this was a truly brilliant meal Mum had got ready for them, she couldn't wait to get back up stairs to it as soon as they were finished.

"Thanks, Mum that was the best!" she gushed. Jamie had his whole face in his bowl trying to lick every last smear of chocolate sauce out of it. "Come on, piggy, you've still got to fill me in on all the school gossip I've missed."

He lifted his face out of his bowl, licked his lips, looked at Aimee, looked down at her bowl, reached across and picked it up and began licking that one out as well. When he had finished he looked up again to see Aimee standing with her mouth agape and Mum shaking her head in disbelief. "What?" he asked; he had been amazed that Aimee had left so much chocolate sauce.

"Come on." Aimee ordered, pulling him to his feet and across to the door.

"I'll do the washing up then shall I?" Mum said without waiting for a reply as they disappeared up the stairs. "Of course I will, because I love doing the washing up don't I? It helps to keep me fit doesn't it? Along with all the other things, shopping and cooking and washing and tidying etcetera, etcetera, etcetera," she muttered as she collected the dishes together.

Jamie lingered on the staircase and called down, "You're talking to yourself again, Mum!"

Aimee smiled as she opened the bedroom door, he really could wind people up without even trying she thought and then she froze, staring at the gull that was sitting on the ledge outside the window, pecking at the pane. It stopped pecking as it realised she was looking at it and turned and tilted its snow-white head to stare at her with its left eye. Its powerful orange beak slowly opened as if it were about to speak to Aimee then closed again as it saw Jamie arriving behind her. With a flurry of white and black wing feathers it took to the sky and quickly disappeared over the rooftops.

"Come on, Sis' out of the way; let's have a look at this bottle of yours before Mum comes hunting for galley slaves to do the washing up!" Jamie said as he pushed past her into the bedroom. He threw himself onto his knees and delved under the bed to retrieve the box. "Hey, it's not there!" he shouted and looked around to catch the expected look of shock on Aimee's face. He did not get exactly what he had expected. Her face was not there, she had gone. He got up and went to the door, she wasn't on the stairs. And then he heard the gulping sobs coming from her bedroom and quietly crept along the corridor to her door.

The door was wide open and he found her kneeling on the floor with her body on the bed, her head covered by her hands, crying. He stood and stared at her, scared and bemused by the effect his 'joke' had had on her. She was shaking as she cried and her hands were pulling at her hair. He closed the door behind him, slowly walked over to her and gently put his hand on her shoulder. She didn't respond to his touch and carried on shaking and sobbing.

"Do you want me to grovel again, Aimee? I'm getting good at it now?" He said and lowered himself to his knees but again got no response. He was finding his big sister's reactions to his jokes worrying. She had always given as good as she got and better! In fact it was usually her that tormented and tricked him. But now look at her, she couldn't even take his weak old 'Oh it's gone!' trick.

"Aimee, Aimee... I'm sorry, Aimee. I don't really know what I've done but I am sorry, honest."

Her shaking subsided a little and she turned her head to look at him. "It's not you, you wombat. It's...it's the gull...the gull at the window!" she whispered between gulps and sobs. "It's gone now," she added as she saw him look up, "But it was there at your window. It's following me and I don't know why. You've got to help me, Jamie!"

She looked him in the eye and he could see her fear. He felt upset at seeing his Aimee like this but also proud that she trusted him enough to help her.

"We'll sort it, Aimee, honestly we will," he said resolutely, "We'll sort it, Sis."

She turned and sat on the floor next to him. "Have you got any tissues?" she asked.

"No, but you can borrow my hanky," he offered, taking it from his pocket and holding it in front of her face.

She looked at the offering. It had obviously once upon a time been a perfectly good pale blue handkerchief, now it might pass for a Victorian chimney sweep's facecloth that had just been rediscovered in an archaeological dig…with signs of recent nasal activity. She declined his offer. "No thanks, I'll get some toilet roll from the bog. Come on, let's get back to the bottle and I'll tell you all I can about the gull."

They went back to Jamie's room via the toilet and he took the box from under the bed. Once again they opened it and took out the brown paper bag. Aimee's hands trembled as she held it. She didn't know why, she didn't remember anything about it. She only knew that Jamie had said that she had been holding it when he found her so it must have something to do with whatever had happened to her. She turned and looked at her brother, "Jamie, come to my room, I want to tell you everything I know before I look in the bag so that if the bottle is important we can both try to make sense of it."

She told him of walking on the beach, calling out in her sleep in hospital and the 'visit' of Dr. Gill. Then she told him about the gull that kept on appearing as if it were following, watching, maybe trying to get her and that it had been there on the roof when they had arrived

27

home.

"And on the window sill when we came into the room last time!" Jamie butted in excitedly, "So it wasn't really me that upset you, it was the gull!"

"Yes…well mostly the gull, you put the icing on the cake with your pratty jokes!"

"Thanks."

Aimee smiled, "So what do you think then?"

"I think that we should look at the bottle and see if it jogs your memory." He nudged her into action and she opened up the bag and pulled the bottle out.

It felt oddly warm as she turned it in her hands, not the usual cool feel of glass. She turned it over and over looking for any writing or symbols or marks. There were none, it was exactly as Jamie had described in the hospital: old looking, square body with a round neck and a marble for a stopper and it had some oily looking liquid in it that seemed to be in layers of different shades of green. At least they were green when she took it out of the bag, now they had changed to more of a blue colour!

"Hey, it's changed colour!" Jamie exclaimed, "Neat trick, Sis!"

"It must be the heat from my hands; it must be heat sensitive whatever it is. Let's try warming it up a bit more." She put the bottle under her arm and snuggled it tightly for a few minutes. "Now let's see…oh, it's still the same blue!" She put it down on the bed and the colour changed back to its original green.

"Here, let me have a go," Jamie said as he picked up the bottle and held it tight. After a minute or so he held it up. It was still green - no change at all. "That's strange! You have another go!"

Aimee picked it up and then dropped it back onto the bed as immediately the oily liquid turned to blue. It wasn't heat sensitive, it was Aimee sensitive!

"That can't happen…can it? I mean it's… impossible…isn't it? Jamie gasped, his eyes telling of the bewilderment he felt. "Here, let me try again!"

He snatched the bottle from the bed and held it gently with his fingertips, then tightly in his right hand, his left hand, in both hands, all with no change in the colour of its contents. "Impossible," he breathed as he gave the bottle to Aimee and watched, eyes agape, as green again became blue.

Aimee held it in her left hand and touched it gently with the fingertips of her right hand. She followed its smooth lines and then again became aware that it was warm to her touch almost as if it was generating its own heat…as if it were alive!

"Impossible!" she agreed as she put it back down on the bed.

"You said I was holding it when you found me. Then it must have something to do with what happened and where it happened or why would I have it?" Aimee reasoned. Jamie nodded his agreement. "So where did I find it and how did I get hurt…and how did I get back home when I was unconscious? I remember setting off for a walk on the beach after you'd gone off to footy practice so perhaps all the dirt came from there. We'll go to the beach first thing tomorrow morning and look for clues." She decided.

"Great and how are you going to wangle me a day off school then genius?" moaned Jamie.

"Oh sorry, I forgot about that. I'll have to wait until you come home. I don't think Mum will let me go on my own yet and I don't really want her to come, she'd only start asking questions and then worry even more about me!"

"Yeh, you should have seen the look on her face when she saw you sprawled all over the doorstep with a massive hole in your h..."

"Thank you Jamie," she interrupted, not wanting to hear the gory bits again even if he did enjoy telling her. She picked up the bottle again which turned instantly blue and radiated its warmth to her hands. "I'd love to be at the beach now..."

The sea water lapped around Aimee's ankles as she stared around at the cliffs. The sky was darkening and a little light rain was just beginning to fall, Aimee shivered and looked down at the bottle, warm in her hands.

"How have I got here?" she whispered to herself though the beach was deserted so no-one could have heard.

She looked up again, following the line of the cliff tops against the late evening sky and saw the newly exposed earth where the edge had broken away and fallen to the beach below to be washed and levelled by the sea. Not a massive slip but enough to bury a twelve year old girl! She walked towards it, her sea-soaked slippers squelching on her feet, her denim jeans clinging to her calves and her thin red t-shirt beginning to darken as it soaked up the rain. Again she shivered, even on a summer evening the wind could be cold coming off the sea, but she also felt frail and confused.

"How have I got here?" she whispered again.

This time she was answered by the screeching cry of the gull as it fell from the sky, diving, wings folded back to allow maximum streamlining and therefore maximum speed. Its wings spread at the last possible moment to control the dive and level off to hit Aimee beak first, to catch and snatch its target.

Aimee's protective reflexes made her turn and bend forward at the very moment the gull stretched out its neck and she felt the disturbed air move over her back and head as it missed. It adjusted its wing shape to make it soar upwards to ready itself for another attack.

She looked up and saw it soaring, gliding and turning, and then it dipped its head, swept back its wings and began its dive.

"Why am I here?" she cried out, "I want to go home!"

Her right leg hit the end of her bed and she pitched forward, her whole body hitting the dry warm duvet a fraction of a second before her head did. Her shivering wet form lay face down for a few moments before she turned over on her back and looked up at the ceiling, eyes wide and staring, trying to make sense of the last few minutes. A familiar voice brought her back to the here and now.

"How the hell did you do that?" Jamie blurted.

"Jamie! What happened? Tell me what happened! I was on the beach and…and the gull…!" Aimee stood up leaving the bottle and her dark sodden imprint on the duvet. She grasped both of his hands tightly and stared into his eyes.

He felt her trembling coldness move up his arms and into his body and he shivered too.

"What happened?" she pleaded.

He looked into his sister's frantic face and suddenly grew up beyond his age. He gently moved her and sat her down on the bed again, speaking calmly and softly to her.

"Ok, Sis, try to calm down. I'll get you a towel… and a drink… and when you're ready we'll go over what happened. We'll work it out, don't worry, we'll do it." He stroked her head being careful to avoid the dressing over her wound that was now struggling to keep its hold.

When he thought she had calmed a little he went through to the bathroom and fetched a large bath towel. "Here, you dry yourself off and get changed while I go down and make us some cocoa," he ordered, "I'll sort your bed out when we've drunk it." She looked up and managed a small smile.

As he passed the lounge door on his way to the kitchen his mum looked up from her magazine and asked, "Are you two alright, I thought I heard a bump a few minutes ago, you've not been fighting again have you. We need to look after Aimee you know."

"Yes, Mum, I know," he smiled. "I'm going to make us some cocoa and then I think she's going to try to get some sleep. I might even read her a bedtime story to help her. See, I'm being a perfect brother to her aren't I?"

She smiled back at him then looked back down at her magazine as she replied, "Yes, a real proper gentleman...I wonder why? You're not trying to get her to do your homework for you I hope!"

"Mum... as if I would!" He did his best to sound shocked at the suggestion.

He made the cocoa, grabbed a handful of biscuits and got back up to Aimee as quick as he could. He didn't want to leave her for long in her fragile state and anyway he was as eager as she was to try and work out what had happened. One second she had been stood by her bed looking at the bottle, the next second she had gone, reappearing a few minutes later shaking and soggy! This was going to take some working out and he was determined to do it.

"Here we are, Sis," he called, as much for Mum to hear as for Aimee and then more quietly, "Get this down you, it will warm you up and help you to calm down a bit." He passed her one of the mugs. She seemed more at ease now and more comfortable in her pyjamas and dressing gown, her hair towelled dry.

"Thanks, Jamie." She gazed down into the mug of swirling creamy brown cocoa, breathing in its rich, sweet, chocolaty steam. "It was real wasn't it? What happened really happened didn't it? I didn't imagine

32

it, did I? I mean… I couldn't have, could I… I got wet didn't I? So how did it happen? I was here… then I was on the beach. I saw the place where I got covered in mud. It's by the cliffs; there must have been a landslip. I saw it and I sort of remembered being there. Then the gull came and it attacked me… perhaps it was what did this to me." She put her hand to the dressing on her head which still needed sticking back into place. "But why… Why would a gull attack me for no reason?"

Jamie took a sip of his cocoa, decided it was still too hot and put it down on the floor by the bed. He leant backwards onto the bed and sat up again almost instantly. He had leant on the bottle. He picked it up and gazed at it, thinking back to Aimee's disappearing act. She had been holding it when she…went. What had she said as it happened? "I'd love to be at the beach now." And she was… she was at the beach! What she wanted to happen… happened!

"What you wanted to happen, happened!" he exclaimed, his face bursting with excited disbelief at the thought of what he had worked out. "Aimee, what you wanted to happen happened! You said you'd love to be at the beach and you were! And you were holding the bottle when you said it! The bottle that changes colour but only when you hold it, not me! The bottle took you to the beach, Aimee!" He held it aloft in a gesture of triumph.

Aimee looked at the bottle, and immediately she knew that it was definitely the smooth thing she had been touching when she was buried. A picture was beginning to form in her mind of the landslip, being buried, scratching at the earth and stones to get out, the gull pecking at her head, ripping into her scalp, touching something smooth and wanting to be home. And she was home, unconscious but home, home for Jamie to find. He was right, he must be right. What else could explain what had happened?

She looked up at her brother, her marvellous brother! "You know what, Dogbreath, I think you're right!"

"You do! Bloody hell!" He picked up his mug of cocoa and drained

33

it in several very large gulps and then gave a burp that anyone would be proud of.

They looked at each other, smiled, and then did what seemed to be the most natural thing to do when a team had triumphed - they hugged each other! After a few seconds they both realised what they were doing and quickly moved apart to each end of the bed.

"Err... you won't tell my mates I just did that will you?" Jamie asked, aware that they could really go to town on him if they knew what he had done.

"Why not, I think it's lovely that you care for your sister so much that you want to cuddle her!" Mum was standing in the open doorway smiling down at them. "In fact if you're not ready for bed within the next five minutes I'll be straight on the phone to Wayne Norton!"

Jamie rushed out of the room and could be heard cleaning his teeth, then getting undressed, his clothes hitting the floor as they were thrown into a corner, and finally the bedsprings creaking as he leapt into bed.

"Night, Aimee...night, Mum, see you in the morning," he called as he hid the bottle under his pillow and imagined the things he would try and get Aimee to agree to do with it. Top of the list involved school and several of its teachers being transported to some far distant planet to do very important missionary work with green gooey things.

"And you could do with a good night's sleep as well. Night night, love."

"Night night, Mum," Aimee smiled as her mum turned off the light and closed the door. She'd give it a half an hour or so and then she'd try out the bottle. Could it really let her do what she wanted? The possibilities were endless but she started making a list of all the things she would like to do, places to go, new things for her and her Mum and even for Jamie...until without realizing it, she was soundly asleep.

But away from the distractions of the waking world, her dream world could be invaded by any creature intent upon creating nightmares…

Swooping down, pecking, and crying out her name…again and again. The sea swirling around her ankles softening the sand and making it so difficult to run, to escape from the razor sharp beak of the gull which swooped and ripped at her flailing arms and hands, trying to get to her head again. She began to sink into the beach, her kicking legs only helping to drag her down further and further until only her head and arms were above the sand and the incoming sea. Her arms were tiring and she needed them now to help keep her head above the water so she dropped them to try to push on the soft sand and the gull saw its chance and landed on her head. She could see its shining black pearls of eyes wide open and staring into her own eyes as if to say, "I have you now, Aimee Hawthorn, I have you now!" And it shrieked in triumph, readying itself for its meal. And Aimee screamed, she drew every last breath of damp, sea-filled air she could into her lungs and she screamed…

The bedroom door hammered open and in stumbled Jamie closely followed by Mum, both anxious to save her from her tormentor, who or whatever it might be.

"Wake up, Sis; you'll scare next doors rottweiler!" Jamie added, trying to be helpful.

"Aimee, Aimee…It's alright love, it's only a dream… Wake up, wake up, Aimee!" Her mum spoke gently yet firmly, taking hold of Aimee's clawing hands and holding them to her sides to avoid being struck.

Aimee suddenly sat bolt upright, her eyes wide and staring at some far distant point. Her mouth opened to take in another lungful of precious air ready to scream.

"AIMEE!" Mum shouted into her face.

Aimee's eyes blinked back into reality but she remained tense, ready to fight… ready to scream. Gradually, as the familiar features of her mum's face forced themselves into her consciousness, her body began to relax. She stiffened again as Jamie switched on the main light and she saw his blurry figure come towards her; only relaxing when she realised it was him as he spoke.

"I think I must have made your cocoa too strong!" he joked, but only as a way of calming himself down. Aimee was beginning to make him feel pretty uneasy!

"I'm sorry, Mum. I was having a horrible dream. I'm sorry if I woke you. I couldn't help it."

"Do you want to talk about it? It might help you to get it out of your mind and let you sleep more easily," Mum asked remembering what the doctor had said on 'Talk to Craig,' her favourite daytime telly programme.

Aimee glanced at Jamie before answering. "Er… no… I er… can't remember much about it now, Mum. It was probably something stupid anyway; you know what dreams are like. I bet it was something that Jamie told me about. He's always talking about weird things isn't he!"

Jamie grinned but changed his face when Mum turned to him and said, "Yes…" in that way that meant she didn't think it was funny, especially at two o'clock in the morning.

"I think I might get back to bed now; School in the morning for some of us you know!" he offered and quickly disappeared back to his room.

"I'll be alright, Mum, honest." Aimee whispered reassuringly.

"If you're sure, love, but if you have any more of those dreams we're going straight back to the hospital with you!"

"Ok, Mum. Go back to bed now and try not to worry about me."

Mum smiled as she turned out the light and Aimee spent the rest of the night waiting for daylight to come, certain that if she slept the gull would come back for her.

Chapter 4

Discoveries

Morning arrived, eventually, along with a hundred songs sung by a friendlier choir of birds than the one that she dreaded. Aimee went to the window as the first rays of sunlight burst into the eastern sky. Pulling the curtains apart just enough to poke her head through she scanned first the garden, then the rooftops and then the sky for the gull. No sign, but of course it could be on her own rooftop and impossible for her to see without going outside! She decided that Jamie could do that before he went to school.

She gazed out across the fields to the cliff tops and the blue-grey sea beyond; calm now after the storms of the last week. The same sea, she thought, that Dad had fished so many times with his crew on the 'Dancing Sally.' She smiled as she remembered him telling her that he named the trawler after Mum because when they were courting he'd taken her to a party at the Manor Court Hotel and she turned out to be an even worse dancer than he was. The same sea that he was supposed to have set sail on when he left home five years ago and never came back. He never even arrived at the docks to get on the boat. He just set off in the car and out of her, their lives. He did leave a letter for her and Jamie, more of a note really:

Dear kids,
> *Sorry I can't face you to say goodbye, I'm a coward that way. I've got to go away. Things are not going very well at the moment and it's for the best that I try and sort things out on my own and not make your lives a misery. I love you all, never forget that, I love you more than you can ever imagine.*
>
> *Dad*

That was it! That was all that he'd written! She had read and re-read it so many times that now she knew it by heart and still, five years later, it hurt her to think that that was all he had to say to her. Her Dad, whom she'd loved so much, couldn't even tell her why he had to go! She knew more than that though. The letter he'd left for Mum told her much more. She'd had to piece together the torn fragments that she'd found in the bin after Mum had read it and raged around, smashing and tearing every picture she could find of him.

Dear Sal,

I'm so sorry. I've kept this from you for so long now, but finally I can't do it any more. The fishing has been really poor for the last few years and I've been borrowing money to keep the boat and crew going. I tried the bank, they were ok at first but when things didn't improve they wouldn't lend any more and I had to try somewhere else. I've been stupid and borrowed from people that you wouldn't want to know. Now they want their money back and more! I can't pay them so I've had to sign the boat over to them; it was either that or the house and I couldn't do that to you and the kids. But then they said that the boat wasn't enough and they wanted more, £50,000 more. They 'suggested' that I should do some jobs for them; boat trips to the continent to pick up "passengers" and "goods." The only way I can see out of this mess is to disappear for a while. If they come looking for me, just tell them the truth – I've gone and you don't know where. I'll get in touch when I've sorted myself out and managed to get some money together, some honest money.

I'll love you always,
Mike

Tears rolled down Aimee's cheeks as she went over the letter again, seeing Dad's handwriting in her minds eye. Five years and he still hadn't been in touch! Had they caught up with him? Where could he be? Why was it taking him so long to come back to them? Was he still… alive? She had thought these thoughts so many times but she could never get closer to any answers. She knew what the "goods" and "passengers" were though. She had been watching the telly with Mum one night after Jamie had been sent to bed for one of his daft tricks, as Mum called them. 'Crime Update' came on and started to go on about drugs and how they were being smuggled into the country on fishing boats, people as well – illegal immigrants they called them. Mum had changed the channel as soon as she realised what they were talking about, but that only made Aimee even more certain that it was what Dad had been caught up in.

The radio alarm come on in Mum's room. A mans voice was talking about the latest inflation figures and she heard Mum groan and turn over in her bed. Aimee smiled; Mum hated mornings. She would stay in bed until midday if she didn't have to go to work. Still it gave her the chance to talk to Jamie about the bottle.

She crept along the landing being careful to avoid the loose floorboard that Dad was always going to fix. Jamie's room smelled of stale gerbil wee, he always had to be forced to clean out Gremlin; he didn't seem to notice the smell himself. She stood at the foot end of the bed and gently lifted the duvet to reveal his feet. He was still wearing his socks which made Aimee smile… until the smell hit her. "He must have been wearing them for weeks," she thought. She was going to tickle his feet but took the more sensible option of pulling the duvet right off him.

"What's going on?" he moaned, "I don't want to get up yet; I need my beauty sleep!"

"You'd have to sleep for years for it to do you any good!" Aimee retorted, "Anyway, we have to talk before Mum gets up. That dream I had last night, it was the gull again. I want you to check around the house before you go to school. I'll make sure I keep the doors and windows closed until you get back this afternoon."

"And make sure you don't let the fire go out or it will come down the chimney!" Jamie grinned.

"We haven't got a chimney; we've got a gas fire!"

"But how does Santa get in then?"

"He doesn't, he sends Rudolph in through the letterbox because he's got a cold so he can't smell your feet!"

"My feet don't smell!" He protested and took one of his socks off and offered it to Aimee.

"Err... after you!" She smiled.

Jamie put the sock to his nose, sniffed in loudly and then looked up at Aimee. "A wonderful aroma!" he lied, then, "Uurgh! I think I feel sick!"

"Hey, Jamie, you've just given me a great idea! How would you like a day off school so we can see if the bottle really does have special powers?" Aimee said excitedly.

"Brilliant idea but how do we get the Mum monster to agree to it?"

"You just lie there and keep smelling the sock; I'll tell Mum that you're feeling ill. Groan a bit, but not too much, we don't want her sending for the doctor." Aimee ordered him, "It's worth a try anyway."

She went through to Mum's room and began to act out the role of concerned sister. "Mum... Mum, I think you should come and look at Jamie. I don't think he's very well. He's been groaning and when I went to see what was up he said he hadn't slept since I woke you both up and that he feels really sick. I'm sorry; it's my fault isn't it."

"Mmm, I think I'll see for myself, he probably just wants a day off school because you're not going!" She replied doubtfully.

Aimee led the way back to Jamie but had to smile into her hand when she saw the look on Mum's face as the smell of the room hit her.

"Alright then, Jamie, where does it hurt?" She asked suspiciously, "I hope you're not putting it on. I know all your tricks me lad, I've had eleven years of them!"

"Ohh... it's my stomach, Mum... and I've got a rotten headache... and..."

"I think that will be enough for starters, Jamie. Alright, I'll ring school up and tell them you won't be in today; your poorly sister can look after you. I'm sure she'll enjoy that! Oh and do me a favour; clean that poor gerbil out and put all your dirty clothes in the washing machine! Make sure he gets it the right way round, Aimee," she smiled as she left the room.

"Good work, Jamie. I'll go and make breakfast and as soon as Mum's gone I'll come back up and we'll get started," Aimee whispered, "See you in a bit."

Three quarters of an hour and several warning instructions from Mum later, they sat on Aimee's bed with the bottle between them and looked at each other.

"Well, what do we do now? Jamie asked, "It only seems to work for you and you daren't leave the house because of your pet gull.

"Some pet, I'd rather have a pet crocodile – at least it wouldn't swoop down out of nowhere at me! If I can't go out of the house I could always try it out around the house; just to find out what I can do with it," Aimee reasoned. She picked up the bottle and, holding it firmly in her right hand, she closed her eyes and said out loud, "I want to go to the kitchen."

When she opened her eyes she was surprised to find Jamie smiling at her; she was still in her own bedroom!

"You either went and came back so fast that I must have blinked and missed it or your bottles run out of juice," he grinned.

"Or perhaps I didn't say the right words. I'll try a different way… Take me to the kitchen!"

She still didn't move.

"I'd like to go to the kitchen… I'd like to go to the kitchen please… Oh I give up! What am I supposed to say? When I went to the beach I just said I'd love to go to the beach and there I was. What am I doing wrong now? I'd love to go to the kitchen so why can't I flipping well go?"

It was Jamie that spotted a possible answer without realising it. "Maybe the bottle doesn't know where the kitchen is." He joked.

"Yes, but it also wouldn't have known where I lived when it brought me home the first time... unless... unless it knew I meant my home. I mean I only have one home, this place, so there couldn't have been anywhere else to bring me could there? There are millions of kitchens aren't there! It might not have understood which one I meant."

"Hey, it would have been really funny if you suddenly appeared out of nowhere right in front of Mrs. Jackson in the school kitchen just as she was putting the lumps in the gravy!" Jamie was rising to the comic possibilities of the bottle.

"I'll try to say exactly where I want to go... Take me to the kitchen in this house..."

And there she was, sat at the kitchen table facing the door. She stood up, went to the cupboard and took out a packet of chocolate digestives. Then she sat down again.

Jamie called out from above, "Aimee, are you there?"

She smiled and said, "Take me back to my bedroom." And as she sat back on her bed she said "No, I'm here silly, have a biscuit!"

"It worked, yes, it worked!" Jamie shouted excitedly punching the air and doing a little dance around the bedroom. "Hey, we can have some real fun now!"

"No, Jamie, we have to use it sensibly, we have to be careful that no one else finds out about it. And there is still the gull! Is it me it's after or the bottle... or both! The trouble is, when I'm alone it comes for me. It doesn't seem to come near when there is someone else around, so if I go off on my own I'll be vulnerable."

"So take me with you!"

"But it didn't change colour for you."

"Yes, but you managed to bring the biscuits back, so if you hold on to me perhaps you can take me with you. Come on, let's try it out. I could do with a cup of tea; bring the biscuits."

"Jamie; you can be almost brilliant at times!" Aimee marvelled and took hold of his right hand in her left, "I want to go back to the kitchen."

"Put the kettle on then, Sis and make your genius of a brother a nice cup of tea," Jamie ordered as he sat down at the table, "Now you've got yourself a bodyguard!"

She didn't even think about arguing, it was such a relief to think that she could use the bottle and take him along as well. As she sat watching Jamie dunking biscuits into his tea and messily filling his mouth with the resulting chocolaty mush she began to have second thoughts. How could someone so irritatingly messy be the one to look after her? And he was her little brother, smart yes, but her little brother all the same. One thing she…they had to do was solve the mystery of the gull; she couldn't go on hiding behind Jamie forever. Then another thought came to her. Why did the bottle only work for her? Another mystery; perhaps they were linked. Maybe if they could find out more about the bottle it would lead them to some answers. Perhaps they should go back to the beach and look around there for clues.

"I think we should go to the beach first and look for clues," Jamie said making Aimee jump.

"How does he do that?" She thought.

They walked back upstairs and went to their rooms to get changed then met up back down in the kitchen.

Aimee loaded her white canvass shoulder bag with biscuits, crisps and a bottle of cola. She put it over her shoulder and held the bottle in her right hand.

"Come on then, Jamie, hold your big sister's hand," she teased.

"Jamie, though, was too excited by the adventure of it all to feel the slightest abashed about holding his sisters hand. Anyway, no one was watching.

"Hang on!" Jamie ran out of the kitchen and returned seconds later carrying his fishing umbrella. "Right, ready!"

"What do you want that for, it's brilliant sunshine out there?"

"But if that gull attacks we can put it up and protect ourselves from its beak… or anything else it might drop on us," he replied, holding his nose.

"You're not just a pretty face are you? Come to think of it you're not even a pretty face. Come on, hold on tight. Take me back to the beach!"

The tide was out and the beach was almost deserted; just a couple walking their dog right at the far end by the rocks and another elderly lady with her dog on the path that lead up to the town. There were hundreds of gulls about; out on the sea, in the air and walking around on the beach. Aimee looked around nervously.

"What kind of gull is it?" Jamie asked.

"I'm not sure; it's big though, bigger than those on the beach… or those in the sky."

"They're mostly black-headed gulls, herring gulls and common gulls. If you say it's bigger than those then it's probably a great black-backed gull. I looked them all up in my bird book when I went to bed last night. All good detectives need to do their research you know."

"Thank you, Sherlock. Black-backed… yes it did have a black back… and a big yellow beak!"

"Yes, it sounds like a black-backed to me. They're scavengers; they'll eat any old bits of meat that they can find so you would have been perfect for it," he grinned, "I can't see any around here now though."

"Good, let's hope it stays that way. Come on, I think that's where the bottle comes from," she said, pointing at the part of the cliff where there was a fresh scar from the land slip, "I think that's what fell on me."

The cliff's mixture of soil, clay and rocks of all sizes was dry now after several hot, sunny days, making it easy for them dig and pull out any interesting pieces of 'evidence.' There were many large, regular shaped pieces of grey stone. Building stone perhaps? And shattered pottery, quite a bit of it. It was mostly brown like the earthenware casserole dish at home, but also some more delicate white pottery with a blue flowery pattern on it. They collected together as much as they could in an old carrier bag that Jamie caught blowing along the beach.

"I haven't done a jigsaw in years," Aimee said as she put another piece of brown into the bag, "Have you still got that tube of super glue that you stuck your fingers together with?"

"Yes, I think it's in my top drawer stuck to the vase I was mending for Mum."

"The one you broke and haven't told her about yet?"

Jamie gave a little grunt and went on scrabbling at the rubble. "Have you noticed that there are loads of bits of charred wood in here?

46

Aimee sat down on one of the larger stones and looked around at their finds. She was becoming more and more convinced that there had once been a building of some kind here, or rather fifteen metres up there on top of the cliff.

"Come on," she called to Jamie, "I want to have a look at the top of the cliff to see if there's anything left up there."

She set off without waiting for a reply and was soon half walking, half jogging her way to the rough cut steps that lead up cliff side. She could hear Jamie calling as she reached the top of the steps and turned; too late to act on the warning he was trying to give her. The great black-backed gull was upon her before she had any chance to defend herself. It gripped her hair tightly in its sharp, webbed claws and flapped its great black wings trying to pull her over the edge of the cliffs. She had been caught by surprise and was off balance. She stumbled almost to the fragile edge before she managed to form the shred of an idea.

Aimee suddenly tucked her legs completely under herself, putting all her weight onto the gull's wings. Powerful as they were, they could not carry her and it was dragged down with her. The pain of having her hair tugged and torn by the gull was made worse by the stretching of her scalp pulling at the stitches in her wound. Several gave way and blood seeped through the dressing and down her forehead into her eyes. Then, as suddenly as it had caught her, the gull let go and with an ear piercing shriek flew off out towards the sea. Aimee dropped forward, her head face down over the crumbling edge of the precipice.

Jamie dropped to his knees at her feet, breathing heavily from his sprint up the cliff steps and from the terror he felt at actually seeing his sister attacked by the gull. He took hold of her ankles and slowly, carefully pulled her back onto safer, more solid ground before turning her over onto her side and into the recovery position he had learnt from watching some medical soap on TV.

"Should I run and ring for an ambulance or would it be better to wait for her to come round and then use the bottle to go back home? If I get the ambulance then how are we going to explain what we were doing out here, instead of being ill at home? How will we explain about her head anyway, nobody would believe us? Even I wouldn't believe us!" he chuntered to himself before deciding to give Aimee a few minutes to recover and then if she didn't he would ring 999. He retrieved the umbrella that he'd thrown at the gull and opened it to provide some shade from the hot summer sun.

As the dark shadow of the umbrella covered her face Aimee stirred and opened her eyes. "I think we'd better go home now," she murmured, "Get the bottle out of my bag."

"Your bag… where is it?" He looked over the edge and saw it lying at the bottom of the cliff and the gull was strutting determinedly across the sand towards it. He quickly picked up a stone and threw it hard. The stone hit the sand in front of the gull making it stop and look up at Jamie. He found another three stones and as he made his way down the steps he threw them every time the gull moved forward. Reaching the bottom step he picked up one more fist sized stone and whooping loudly charged at the gull, his right arm bent back ready to throw.

The gull spread its black wings and, flapping frantically, rose up from the sand to escape the mad child coming at it. It flew in a circle above Jamie then up to where Aimee lay defenceless on the cliff edge.

Jamie grabbed the bag and ran back up the steps shouting, "Aimee, Aimee!" When he reached the top of the steps he was surprised to find no trace of the gull. "Are you ok, Aimee?" he gasped as he collapsed to his knees by her side.

"I think my head's going to explode but otherwise I think I'm alright. Have you found the bottle?"

"The bottle? Yes, well I've got your bag that is," and he looked at the bag. It was stained a ruddy brown colour and drops of liquid

48

dripped from it onto the grass. He quickly pulled the zip open and gazed down into it. "Oh no," he moaned.

"What is it? Is it smashed? Jamie, let me have a look," Aimee pleaded sitting up and pushing the umbrella to one side.

"You're not going to like it, Sis," he said quietly as he handed the bag to her.

Her hands began to shake as she took it from him and put it on the floor.

"The crisp bag has popped, the biscuits are all broken and the cola bottle has split and made a real mess of the lot of it," Jamie whined before dropping his act and smiling broadly at Aimee, "The bottle seems intact though!"

"You rotten pile of rat droppings, why do you have to always make me suffer like that?"

"Because you're my sister and it's what I'm good at. Come on; let's get home and sort out your head, it's leaking again." He pulled her up onto her feet and held her firmly around the waist as she wobbled unsteadily.

Aimee took the bottle from her bag and wiped it on his shirt and was surprised that he didn't complain. She looked closely at it to check for damage but it was Jamie that noticed that the liquid inside was glowing and changing colour from deep orange to the brightest of yellows and back again. They both stared at it, transfixed by its beauty until finally Aimee broke the spell by overbalancing and nearly pulling both of them to the ground.

"I think I need to go home now Jamie," she said quietly and then a little louder, "I want to go home."

In an instant they were back in the kitchen again and Jamie quickly sat his sister down at the table. One look at the blood soaked dressing on her head was enough to convince him that she needed to see a doctor. He went to the telephone in the hallway, rang Mum's work number and asked the receptionist for Mrs Hawthorn. When she came on the line she knew immediately that something was wrong.

"Hello, Mum, er… I'm afraid Aimee's had a bit of an accident. She sort of went a bit dizzy and fell against the door in the kitchen. I think she might need to have her stitches looked at again."

Mum's voice was a mixture of concern and annoyance, "I'll ask if I can have the afternoon off. If I find that you've done it with one of your stupid tricks I'll murder you, Jamie! I'll be home as soon as I can."

"Did you hear what I told Mum? We have to get our stories straight so she doesn't twig what we've been up to," he said as he returned to the kitchen, but Aimee didn't hear. She had her head down on the table and was soundly asleep. "Ah well, I suppose it's up to me then."

He took the bottle from the bag, went up to his room and secreted it in his 'place that no one will ever find'; in an old sock under the wardrobe. Then he returned to the kitchen and emptied the crisp, biscuit and cola soup out of Aimee's shoulder bag into an old carrier bag and took it out to the bin. He squeezed washing up liquid into and all over the shoulder bag, filled the sink with warm water and gave it a feverish scrubbing, then rinsed it under the tap and put it outside on the washing line to dry. He took off both his own and Aimee's shoes and emptied them of sand out on the garden before replacing them. Standing by the kitchen door he looked around the room as he knew his Mum would, looking for anything out of place that could incriminate them. And finally he smiled at a job well done and just in time as he heard the car draw up on the driveway outside.

As the car door slammed shut he noticed that Aimee's hands were still covered in the reddish-brown dirt from the cliffs. He leapt to the sink, doused a pan scrubber in washing up liquid and water and began to scrub away at them as Mum's key clinked into the front door lock. He threw the scrubber back into the sink and quickly wiped his and her hands dry on a tea towel, dropping it to the floor and kicking it under the table as Mum entered.

"You go to your room, get changed into some decent clothes and wash your face; we're taking Aimee straight to the hospital!"

"Yes Mum. It wasn't my faul…"

"Now!"

She gently roused Aimee and led her out to the car, carefully sitting her in the back seat and fastening the seat belt around her. Jamie came thumping back down the stairs, locked the front door and joined them.

It was twenty minutes later when they were sat in the Accident and Emergency department awaiting their turn that Mum finally started to relax a little and ask what happened.

"It was like I said on the phone, Mum, Aimee and me went to the kitchen to make ourselves some tea and she just went all wobbly like. She fell over into the door before I had the chance to do anything. That's right isn't it, Aimee?"

"Err… I think so," Aimee replied without looking at Mum.

"If I find out there's been any monkey business I'll ground you both for the rest of the summer you know!" Mum warned. "Anyway, you'll be back at school tomorrow, Jamie and I've asked if I can take the next two weeks off as holiday so I'll take care of you now, Aimee."

"Thanks, Mum," Aimee responded half-heartedly. She had so much that she wanted to find out about the bottle and the cliff building but now all that would have to wait until school finished and Jamie was at home to be with her. Her head started to throb with pain again and she decided it might be for the best that she let her head heal up before she ventured back to the beach.

"Aimee Hawthorn, we're ready to see to you now," the nurse called from one of the white curtained cubicles.

Aimee and her Mum stood up. Jamie stood up too but was pushed back down by Mum. "You wait there; I don't want you gawping while Aimee is being treated!"

"Aww, Mum… I could help. I'm brilliant at threading needles you know."

"Sit there and try not to cause chaos for a change please," Mum smiled.

"I'll ask for the old stitches for your collection if you like," Aimee grinned as she went through the curtains.

Chapter 5

Research

The next two weeks were very frustrating as Aimee was confined to the house and garden and was continually fussed over and organised by Mum. DC Martin called to tell them the mud was from the cliffs and as Aimee had not remembered anything else they presumed she must have taken a tumble whilst out on her walk. Otherwise she spent the whole of the first week trying to get some time on her own to find out more about the bottle's powers. She knew where Jamie had hidden it, his secret places never were that secret, but daren't go near it in case Mum found her with it. Even if she did manage to get some freedom she daren't use it on her own because of the gull.

By the start of the second week she had hit on the idea of sending Jamie to the library to find some books on local history so she could see if they mentioned anything about there being a building on the cliff top. They knew Jamie well at the library because he enjoyed reading ghost and horror stories and they would order books from other libraries for him when he'd read all the ones they had. Libraries are good like that.

Mr. Phillips the chief librarian turned out to be a keen local historian and supplied Jamie with information and old maps of the area as well as some really good books. They included one that got Jamie really excited called, 'The Scowcroft Mystery,' that told the story of strange goings in the area four hundred years ago. Although Mum was puzzled by their sudden interest in local history she could see no harm in it and as it kept them occupied and out of her hair she was really quite pleased.

The Scowcroft Mystery turned out to be even more interesting than they could have imagined, especially when they began to link it with the other information they were beginning to gather together. Scowcroft was a house surrounded by a tall stone wall on the northern edge of the town. It was built by the Larus family who had been the main landlords, law makers and law enforcers of the area since King John ruled the land. They were not a very nice family and made sure they kept their hold on their "subjects" by using paid thugs to do brutal things to anyone who got above themselves. The 'Mystery' was that the whole family disappeared one night leaving the town to rule itself. No trace was ever found of Lord Larus, his wife or of any of his five children. When their servants had finished their chores and settled in their lowly rooms for the night, all was as normal. The next morning they went to rouse their master for breakfast but he and his family were gone. There was no sign of any struggle and nothing was missing. Jamie was well and truly hooked by this story. Aimee had other things on her mind.

One of the documents that Mr. Phillips had photocopied for them showed a register of the names and addresses of all the tenants of Lord Larus. When they matched this with one of the maps they discovered that there was a property; a cottage with a large garden, sited near to the cliffs and occupied by someone called Thomas May. Aimee opened up the Ordnance Survey map of the area that had belonged to Dad and, by matching up the old roads and bridle paths on both maps, quickly saw that Thomas May's cottage would today be right on the cliff's edge. It would in fact be exactly where the cliff had crumbled away on top of her. The remnants of the cottage were probably the charred wood and building stone that they had found in the land slip. The pottery could have once belonged to Thomas May… and the bottle? They now had a name and a building to concentrate on.

Aimee decided that she needed to get out and investigate Scowcroft House, the path and most of all the site of May's cottage; but it was still only Wednesday and Jamie wouldn't be free until Friday. And even then Mum was sure to be watching them like a hawk until she trusted them again. So she did the next best thing and instructed Jamie to find out what he could about Scowcroft by asking around at school and walking that way back home after school.

Once again Jamie was up to the task. By Thursday he had discovered that the house was owned by George Walmsley who also owned the, 'Red House Hotel; and, 'The Harbour Inn.' He drove a big black 4x4 pick up truck, was covered in gold chains, smoked big cigars and was going bald. His wife was called Fiona and had blond hair and wore skimpy dresses that she didn't quite fit into any more. Both of them were very suntanned and spoke in loud voices.

"That's brilliant, Jamie, how on earth did you manage to find out so much so quickly?" Aimee asked, wide eyed at the depth of information he had uncovered in just one day.

"I keep telling you that I'm an ace detective," he smiled conceitedly.

"Come on, how did you do it?" Aimee persisted.

"Well… actually…"

"Yes, come on, spill the beans."

"The Walmsleys have got a son called Jordon and he goes to our school. You've probably seen him around, he's in the year above me and he always has his little gang around him. You know who I mean, gelled up black hair, wears gold bracelets and he's about ten sizes bigger than anyone else."

"Not that slimeball who's always pushing in the dinner line and sweats a lot!" Aimee screwed up her face and shivered at the thought of him.

"You've got him, I think he quite likes you; he always pushes in just behind you," Jamie smirked.

"That's because he tried to push in in front of me once and I told him that if he didn't get to the back I would hold his hand and take him there!" She smiled.

"Did he go?"

"Oh yes, he went; I don't think he realised just how strong a grip I've got. He went a lovely shade of red as well. So that's who he is. Mmm, not much chance of getting him to invite us to tea then," Aimee mused, "We'll have to find another way in."

By the end of a second week of Aimee and Jamie's perfect polite and helpful behaviour Mum's nerves could stand no more. On the Saturday morning she let them out, "Just to the shop. And make sure you go straight there and come straight back. No detours, got it?"

"Yes, Mum, thanks, Mum. Do you want us to bring you anything? Some chocolate perhaps?" Aimee asked pulling out all the stops to gain as much freedom as possible.

"Some chocolate would be nice," Mum admitted and off they went.

At the end of the drive Jamie took hold of his sister's arm and smiled at her, "She didn't say which shop did she? We could go to the one that's sort of near to Scowcroft. If we were quick that is," and he took the bottle from down his trousers.

"Jamie! I hope you remembered to change your underpants this morning." Aimee protested, but marvelled at his scheming. She took the bottle and pulled Jamie behind the holly bush in the corner of the front garden. Satisfied that they were hidden from anyone's view she ordered the bottle to; "Take me to the front gate of Scowcroft House."

Once there they walked around the walls that kept the house prisoner until they reached the path that led to the cliff steps. Where the path started there was a change of brickwork in the wall; it was obvious that there had once been an entrance there. Another piece for the jigsaw! They continued around the walls until they were back where they started. It had taken them several minutes to complete the circuit; it was a sizeable property. Once they had bought their magazines, sweets and of course chocolate from the nearby shop they found a quiet alleyway and used the bottle to return home.

Mum was surprised to see them back so soon. They really were being too good to be true, but she decided to make the most of it while it lasted. "Well done you two, if you can keep this up I might let you go for a walk this afternoon," she smiled.

Aimee smiled back at her and turned to go up to her room when she was stopped in her tracks by Mum's next remark.

"By the way, where did you get the bottle from? It's very unusual, did you find it somewhere?"

In their delight at having been out and discovered more interesting information they had forgotten to hide the bottle and Aimee had simply walked in with in her hand. She held the bottle up and looked at it. "Err... yes, I found it on the beach a few months ago and left it in the garden. I've just remembered it. I thought I'd polish it up and keep it in my room. Pretty isn't it?"

"Lovely, dear; another piece of junk to clutter up the place!" Mum replied dubiously.

Up in Aimee's bedroom they spread out the old maps on the bed. The path went along the coast to Beemouth now, but on the old maps it only went as far as the top of the steps where the ruins are. They threw ideas at each other as to why there should be a gate and a path going from Scowcroft to the cliff tops. For nice walks? To go up to the cliff top to look out to sea? To take prisoners to be thrown off the cliffs? That was one of Jamie's. The most likely one seemed to be that the ruined cottage was connected to Scowcroft for some reason.

"Perhaps it was a holiday cottage?" Jamie suggested.

"Holiday cottage, the only holidays they had in those days was to go off and steal someone else's country! Anyway, we know the cottage was occupied by Thomas May, he was one of Lord Larus' tenants remember. So why did Larus have a special path to Thomas May... and don't say, "To collect the rent." I think we have to find out a bit more about this Thomas May chap. Pass me the big blue book, you look in the green one."

After a long period of quiet, broken only by deep sighs from Jamie that meant he wanted another sweet, Aimee slammed her book shut and announced, "All I can find about Thomas May is that he was some sort of doctor who made medicines from herbs and did a lot of studying the stars."

"Mine says he was a supposed to be a sage or something and he would only come down to the town if anyone was ill," Jamie added.

"Not much to go on is there?" Aimee sighed. She picked up the bottle from the bedside table and stared at it as it changed colour from green to blue in her hands. "Hey, wasn't it glowing orange up on the cliff?"

"Yes, yes it was!" Jamie confirmed.

"So why is it green or blue here? It must have some connection with the cottage on the cliff. Perhaps that's where it came from," Aimee guessed, "Oh I'd love to go back in time and see that cottage as it was when Thomas May lived there."

The bedroom disappeared and in front of her was a grey, stone-built building with a stone tiled roof and small glassless openings for windows that had wooden shutters at each side. She was by an opening in the low garden wall, by the path that led down to Scowcroft; she could see its roof down the hill.

A large man with long wavy black hair came out of the door and strode towards the opening. As he reached it he turned back towards the cottage and shouted angrily, "You'll have it ready by tomorrow or I'll have her chained to the rocks!" Then he turned back towards where Aimee stood walked straight past her as if she wasn't there and away down the path.

Aimee watched him go, amazed that he hadn't even glanced at her, and then she turned towards the cottage again and slowly walked towards it. She glanced down at the bottle and again it was glowing, orange and yellow. As she reached the doorway she paused as it suddenly came to her; the man she had seen was wearing a long black cloak and knee length boots. She had travelled in time. This was Thomas May's cottage and he would be inside!

Cautiously, she crept inside the doorway and stood trying to adjust her eyes to the gloomy, smoky room. Besides the little window only the fire at the far side of the room gave any light to the place. In the middle of the room was a large solid looking wooden table with two equally solid chairs. In one of the chairs sat bent over with his head in his hands was an old man with a balding head fringed with matted, straggly grey hair.

He suddenly stood up from the table sending the chair tumbling backwards to the wall behind. He turned and stared at the doorway where Aimee still stood. Her whole body froze as he stared at her. Then she realised he wasn't staring at her, he was staring through her, away to where the other man had gone. He couldn't see her; the other man couldn't have seen her!

"You'll not get what you want from me, Larus, not now, not ever," he spoke in a soft but firm voice, "But you will get what is coming to you I swear. In my Martha's name I will make sure you get what you deserve." Then he walked to the doorway and shouted, "YOU WILL GET WHAT YOU DESERVE, LARUS!"

Aimee couldn't hold her nerve much longer having him stood right by her side and it snapped when he raised his arm and leaned on the door post, right where she stood, his arm going straight through her! He immediately stood up straight again and backed away as if he had touched something unpleasant. He looked thoughtfully at the doorway before turning to pick up the chair and return to his place at the table.

Aimee held up the bottle and hoped she could find the right words. "Take me back to my time, to my bedroom."

59

"I wish you'd let me know when you're going to disappear on me. It throws me a wobble when you suddenly go like that. Where have you been anyway? I thought you daren't go anywhere without me. No gull this time then?" Jamie greeted her return.

"How long have I been gone?" Aimee asked after several wit gathering seconds.

"About five minutes."

"Five minutes; that's about right. I went where I said I wanted to go, to Thomas May's cottage. And he was there, Jamie! And something was going on... I think Lord Larus was there too. But they couldn't see me... except I think Thomas May knew I was there because of the way he looked at me. I've travelled in time, Jamie!" Aimee gabbled, as she sat down wild eyed and excited on the bed.

"In time... we can have some proper fun now, Sis!"

Chapter 6

Ghosts

"Aimee, Jamie, come down your lunch is ready," Mum called from the kitchen, "Quick now before it goes cold."

They looked at each other fleetingly, stood up and raced down the stairs. They both realised that the sooner they finished their meal, the sooner they could go on their "walk." They were careful though to stop at the bottom of the stairs and walk calmly into the kitchen. They didn't want Mum to change her mind, though Jamie perhaps overdid it a little by stopping at the door and allowing Aimee past saying, "After you, my lady."

Mum smiled at that but Aimee detected a look of suspicion in her eyes as she commented, "Well aren't we the polite one all of a sudden?"

The beans on toast did not last very long, but then it never did being one of their favourites. Jamie once again ended up with tomato sauce all around his mouth and on the tip of his nose after he had licked his plate clean. And Mum seemed to relax a bit as if Jamie being his usual piggy self made things more normal. They managed to take their time over their strawberry yoghurts, but again Jamie went over the top by saying, "Well that was a lovely lunch, Mum; please may we leave the table now?"

"I think I prefer you being your usual horrible self," Mum smiled, "All right, you two can go out but I want you back here no later than five o'clock. Any later and you'll both be grounded again! And do try to keep out of bother; it can't be that hard surely."

"Yes, Mum, thanks, Mum," they chirruped as they rose from the table and made for the door.

"Jamie!"

Jamie stopped and slowly turned around with a worried look on his face. "Yes, Mum?" He asked with a catch in his voice.

"Wash your face before you go, vegetable beans belong in tomato sauce not human beans!"

Jamie sighed with relief then saw the pun and smiled broadly. "Yes, Mum…thanks, Mum…see you later, Mum," he called as he ran up the stairs to get ready for an afternoon of adventure.

Aimee was waiting for him at the top of the stairs. "Hurry up, get washed and don't forget to bring that umbrella, it came in handy last time."

"Ok, Sis, I'll only be a minute…have you got the bottle?"

"Of course I have dimple brain, it's in my bag. And I've wrapped it in a jumper in case of accidents."

"Good idea, knowing what you're like," he replied and skipped into the bathroom to let his face look at the water before he wiped the sauce off on the towel.

Two minutes later they were on the path heading for the gate, Mum watching them from the kitchen window and giving them a little wave which they returned with a smile.

"Where are we heading for then?" Jamie asked as they rounded the corner out of sight.

Aimee wasn't listening; she had spotted a gull on Mrs Addison's rooftop and was trying to decide if it had a black back.

"Aimee… Aimee," he persisted then followed her gaze up to the gull. "It's ok, that's just a herring gull; yours is much bigger."

"Thanks, Jamie, that's a real comfort!"

"Well, where are we heading for then?"

Aimee thought for a few moments and then said decisively, "Back to the cliff top, I want to go back and see Thomas May again. I am sure he's got something to do with the bottle. I want to find out as much about it as I can so I know how to use it properly."

"I'd sort of hoped we could have gone forward in time and found out tonight's winning lottery numbers so we could tell Mum to buy the winning ticket," Jamie tried.

"Well the bottle's mine so we go to the cottage."

"But can we do my idea when we get back?" He persisted.

"Maybe, if we find out all we need to, ok?"

"Ok, Sis, you're the boss."

"And don't you forget it!"

They reached the top of the cliff steps without any sign of the gull and sat down on the grass as Aimee outlined her plan.

"We're going to go back to Thomas May's time, to when Larus is there so we can find out what was going on between them. They had had some sort of argument about something that Larus wanted and May didn't want him to have, I want to find out what it was."

"And you're certain they won't be able to see us?" Jamie asked a little nervously. "Only I don't really like the sound of this Larus bloke."

"I'm not certain, but I don't think so, not Larus anyway. Besides, I thought you were the great adventurer, the 'Indiana Jones' of

Ebbmouth High School, now you're sounding more like Wimpy the Wimp from Wimpville Wimps Academy!"

"I just don't want to be thrown off a cliff that's all, I'm too young and beautiful to die," he replied and grinned a forced grin, "Come on then, Sis, lets do the time warp yeh."

Aimee took the bottle from her bag, held it firmly in her right hand and took hold of Jamie's right hand with her left. "Now," she looked into Jamie's eyes as she spoke, "I want you to watch everything and listen to everything. Don't say a word in case they can hear you and don't wander away from me. If we have to come back quickly I want you right by my side where I can grab you, got it?"

"Yes, Sis."

"Good, now let's see if I can get the wording nice and precise so we arrive at the right place, at the right time. I want to go back to Thomas May's time like I did earlier but just as Lord Larus arrives."

The scene around them changed as she spoke the last word. They were still at the top of the steps but now, there in front of them stood the stone cottage of Thomas May.

"It worked!" yelped Jamie in astonishment.

"Those are your last words, ok?" Aimee threatened and then froze, staring down the steps at Lord Larus as he climbed them purposefully. She pulled Jamie along towards the cottage and went down the garden path to stand by the door ready to enter when Larus got there.

Larus approached the cottage, took a large and very sharp looking dagger from under his cloak and hammered on the door with its handle. "May, May… open up, I know you're in there!"

They could hear footsteps from inside the cottage and then the sound of two heavy bolts being slid back and slowly the rough timbered door swung creakily open. Wood smoke drifted out of the widening gap in the doorway followed by Thomas May who squinted and blinked in the late morning sunlight. As his eyes became accustomed to the light he forced a smile, brushed down his shabby wool and animal skin clothes with his hands and bowed his head slightly, "Ah, Lord Larus, you do me great honour by visiting me this fine summer's morning."

"I am here to see what progress you have made, I am growing impatient and your wife is growing thin in my dungeon!" Lord Larus snarled.

"My wife is a strong woman and will resist you with all of that strength. And she knows that if you harm her then I will make sure you pay dearly for it," May replied calmly and sincerely.

"And your son; you might have sent him away from here but I have my men out searching for him. That and a reward for his capture will bring him to me soon enough. I hope for his sake that you are able to complete the task I have set for you. Now let me see how far you have progressed," and he pushed his way past May into the gloom of the cottage.

Thomas May then did something that sent a shiver through both Aimee and Jamie's bodies; he looked straight at them, nodded his head, smiled and beckoned to them to come inside. He could see them!

They followed him in and stood just inside the doorway, their backs against the cold stone wall. Jamie's hand gripped Aimee's so tightly that it hurt but she was glad to have him there as they watched the two men conduct their business by a workbench nestled in the corner of the room.

Aimee looked around and saw details she had missed in her last hurried visit. The workbench was one; another was the wooden bed frame with its rough straw mattress and woollen blankets. There were no other doors in the room apart from those of a large wooden dresser at the opposite side to the bed. This was where Thomas May, his wife and son lived, ate and slept - one room for all their needs. The workbench meant he worked there also; the bunches of plants hanging from the roof beams and around the fireplace for his healing potions.

"So, have you managed to gain entry into the Star Fall yet? I want the power it brings… I want to know the secrets it holds. You are the only one with the knowledge to bring them to me and the lives of your wife and son depend on you. Let me see the progress you have made." Larus ordered.

"I have made progress, but none that will give you satisfaction. I have weighed and measured it. I have tested it with alkahest. I have subjected it to great heat. And all my work has taken me closer to understanding the truth of the Star Fall but you will remain ignorant until I see my Martha safe inside these four walls again."

Larus grew angry at these words; he was used to getting what he wanted. He was used to men that obeyed without question. He was not used to being told what would happen and what <u>he</u> would have to do!

"I have had enough of your impudence, May. I want to know the power of the Star Fall by noon tomorrow or your precious Martha will die!" shouted Larus and he stormed out of the cottage pausing at the opening in the garden wall to turn and continue, "You'll have it ready by tomorrow or I'll have her chained to the rocks for the sea to claim!"

May's reaction was just as it was when Aimee had been there earlier, but as he leant on the doorpost he sighed and turned to look towards them. "I see you have brought your brother with you this time. I hope our Lord Larus' little tantrum hasn't made you want to leave so quickly as you did before; I should like to talk to you a little, my dear."

"You can see us… then why couldn't he see us?" Aimee asked the question that was in both her and Jamie's mind.

"Ah, there are many things that you have to know, that only I can explain. Just as there are many things that you know of the future that I do not know and must not be told."

"Why not?" Jamie asked. He was puzzled as to why such a useful source of information shouldn't be used.

"The future must always be seen when it happens and never before its time," May replied enigmatically. "Now come and sit at my table and ask your questions." He picked up the chair he had overturned and sat himself down with them. "You must pardon my loss of temper but that Larus would make a sinner out of a saint."

Jamie couldn't get the thought of winning the lottery out of his mind and asked, "If you knew what was going to happen in the future and you didn't like it you could make it happen differently couldn't you?"

"And what if the changes you made to make things happen differently actually made things even worse?" May answered with a frown.

"Yes, but surely winning the lottery wouldn't be worse!" Jamie blurted out.

Aimee gave him one of her, "If you open your mouth again then I am going to close it for you!" hard stares.

"Lottery? What is this 'lottery' you talk of?" May replied looking puzzled.

"Ignore him, Mr May, his brain doesn't work his mouth sometimes. But one thing does confuse me; if you don't know about the future then how do you know about us?" Aimee asked.

May sat back in his chair and smiled, "Now that is a very good question, the first of many I am sure. You see… I am sorry; I do not know your names."

"Aimee Hawthorn and this is my little brother, Jamie," Aimee replied putting extra emphasis on the little.

"Aimee and Jamie, such a lovely rhyme… Aimee Jamie, Jamie Aimee… and Hawthorn; how apt that you should bear that name."

"Why apt?" Aimee asked.

May stared up at the ceiling for a moment before answering. "What I am about to tell you must always remain a secret between the three of us. Is that understood?"

Aimee nodded and said, "Yes." Jamie merely nodded.

"I said; it must remain a secret." He looked straight and hard into Jamie's eyes, "And I do have ways of making sure secrets are kept, Jamie Hawthorn!"

"Yes, yes I'll keep it secret… honest I will. I will, won't I, Aimee?"

"He'll keep it secret, Mr May, I'll vouch for that."

"Good. Now I will begin my story. My father's father built this house when he grew weary of travelling and decided to settle here with his wife. It was he that began the tradition of healing with herbs and potions that I carry on to this very day. It was also he that from his travels brought back knowledge and skills from many lands to be used for the benefit of mankind. Here, in this very room, he made cures for poor and rich alike but only taking payment from the rich," he smiled with pride. "He also worked with base elements to produce new materials and studied the stars to learn more of their secrets. His wife meanwhile had given him a son, my father, to whom he passed on his knowledge, his thirst for new discoveries and his soul. My father also travelled to distant lands old and new, continually learning all he could before he returned here to carry on the good works of his father. He also brought back a wife, and she brought me into this world to carry on his work. When my father could teach me no more I was sent on my way to discover what I could from lands far and near and told only to return when I knew the time was right. Alas I returned two years too late! Lord Larus had put his sword to my parents when my father had failed to save the life of his father who had fallen from his horse whilst out hunting. He had also stolen this house. I had to pay to rent it from him so that I could continue the work of my father and provide a home for my new wife, Martha."

Tears trickled from Thomas' eyes and he sighed deeply before continuing. "And so it was that Larus became my enemy, but an enemy who knew of my learning and needed me when, after fifteen uneasy years as a neighbour, he found the Star Fall and yearned for its secrets. He also knew that I would not help him willingly so he stole away my Martha and would have also taken our son, Francis, had I not already sent him away. That is why I know that Larus will not find him; he is no longer within these shores."

"But what will you do to save Martha? Will you give him the secrets of the... the Star Fall?" asked Aimee anxiously.

"I have a plan. A plan that involves the secrets I have discovered within the Star Fall. You see I spoke the truth about the tests I made on it... but I did not tell of all of my discoveries." He stood up and went over to the dresser, opened one of its doors, took out a football sized silvery blue-grey sphere and placed it on the table.

"Can you see what I discovered?" May asked them and stood back to watch their puzzled faces as they investigated the sphere.

It seemed to have no sign of an opening or indeed any means of unscrewing a panel to gain entry. Its surface wasn't smooth though; it was randomly pitted all over and reminded Aimee of the surface of the moon with its craters. It was Jamie that spoke first, saying something that was really very obvious when you thought about it, but something that Aimee had completely missed. "I don't think it's a natural object, I think it has been made by someone... someone out there in space."

"The Jamie does have a mind after all!" May declared in wonderment.

Then Aimee noticed that four of the 'craters' formed a sort of semi-circle and each one looked to be the size of a fingerprint. She leant across and placed her fingers on the craters and was startled when the top third of the sphere suddenly started to turn on its own and then pop apart from the bottom two thirds revealing an empty compartment in the centre.

"Well done, Aimee Hawthorn, well done my child," May congratulated her, "Well done both of you. This container has protected and imprisoned a special secret in its journey to Earth, and now I shall tell you about it."

He returned to the cupboard and took out two leather bags each about the size of a bag of sugar and brought them to the table, placing them at the side of the sphere. He opened the first and took out a bottle exactly like the one that Aimee now had in her shoulder bag. Its contents glowed orange and yellow just as Aimee's bottle had done on the cliff top. From the other bag he took a flat based round glass container with a wide top and glass stopper. Inside this was more of the glowing liquid.

"Let me explain why I have two containers for the contents of the sphere: When I opened the sphere this liquid was in one round black container with a sealed stopper that I had to break to enter. I decided straightaway that if I had to give some to Lord Larus then I must keep some for myself. Hence the two containers, mine is the sealed one. I learnt how to make glass from my father but the design of the bottle and its sealed sphere stopper came from my travels in the eastern lands. This is the reason I sealed it so soundly,"

He held up his left hand and they noticed for the first time that his little finger was shortened to the first joint.

"I tested the liquid with my finger and this is the result. It just seemed to melt away into it and yet I felt no pain just a gentle warmth. I tested the other with my writing quill and it went the same way. It was as I went to put the two containers away that I discovered the secret power - the one that has brought you to see me here today. I was carrying them to the cupboard when I suddenly felt a great yearning to see my Martha and I spoke out loud, "Oh Martha, I would dearly like to be by your side." And there I was, in Lord Larus' dungeon right beside my lovely wife. At first I didn't realise what had happened and thought I must be dreaming, but when she turned and kissed my cheek I knew it was real and that it must be the power of the liquid that had worked such magic! I of course tried to return with her, holding her hand and wishing to come home but only I returned. The chains must have held her there and the power would work for me only." He put his head in his hands and began to cry gently to himself.

"But why does it work for me and you and not for anyone else?"

"Ah," he looked up and wiped his eyes, "I have thought hard on that since I saw you in the doorway and I think I have an answer. You see when I lost my finger in the liquid I think I became part of the liquid. Perhaps only those that carry my blood can use the power.

"Yes but how am I the same blood as you? Aimee narrowed her eyes trying to think of the answer to her own question. It came to her just as Thomas was about to give his reply. "Unless you are one of my ancestors… but then why does it only work when I hold it and not Jamie?"

"Yes, I was thinking that." Jamie chipped in.

"I think that it may be only the first born of each generation that the real power passes on to," May suggested, "It seems the mysteries of the Star Fall are never fully understood."

"Flipping typical, I miss out again!" Jamie moaned.

"Are you going to give the other liquid to Larus and get Martha back?" Aimee asked ignoring her brother's sulk.

"Yes, yes I think I will. As I said, I have a plan and if all goes well by this time tomorrow I will have Martha by my side and Lord Larus will bother us no more," May smiled as he carried out his plan in his mind. "Come with me my friends… my family."

71

He led them out into the garden with its neat little rows of growing herbs and stopped by the wall in the furthest corner from the cliffs. He bent and lifted a heavy stone from beside the base of the wall to reveal a small square hole lined with grey metal. He looked up at them and said, "I know that you must return to your own time soon and I would not want you to see what happens if my plan comes to fruition. But I will write it down, and more, so that you will learn of how I dealt with our evil Lord. I will place the letter in a jar and leave it here for you to find. Make sure you use your power well and may it bring you peace and happiness, Aimee and Jamie Hawthorn. Hawthorn ha!" he laughed.

"What's so funny about Hawthorn? Why did you say it was apt, you haven't told us yet," Jamie complained.

"See if you can work that one out for yourselves when you get home. Now go before your mother misses you."

Aimee took out the bottle, took hold of Jamie's hand and was about to ask to return when Jamie thought of one more question that May had not answered, "How come you can see us but no one else can?"

"Ah, questions, questions... because they are not of your bloodline of course and even I only see you vaguely. You are mere wisps of shadows to my eyes, like ghosts that come to haunt me pleasantly," he smiled.

Aimee made her request and they were back on the cliff tops with Jamie's tummy rumbling loudly.

"It must be nearly teatime by the sound of it, come on Dogbreath, let's see if there's anything in our post-box."

They looked around at where the garden wall would have been, it was just a raised mound of earth now, and followed its contours until they got to where they thought was the corner of the garden. After some kicking away of grass and earth they uncovered the heavy stone and with some effort managed to prise it loose. There in its box was a brown earthenware jar with a lid sealed with wax.

Aimee carefully lifted the jar from its resting place and put it into her bag alongside the bottle. "Let's go home now, we've had a lovely time on the beach haven't we?" she said with a wink.

Chapter 7

Letter

Saturday tea at the Hawthorns was always fish and chips with mushy peas and today was no exception. As soon as they walked in through the front door Mum called them in to the kitchen, gave them the money and sent them back out again to fetch the feast from 'Charlie's Chippy' just along the road.

"Brilliant, I'd forgotten it was Saturday… fish and chip night," Jamie sighed and closed his eyes and lifted his nose to the aroma coming from the shop, "Mmmm…"

"You know, if your brain was as big as your belly you'd be a child genius," Aimee teased but she had to admit that her own stomach couldn't wait much longer judging by the noises it was making.

There were nine people in front of them in the queue at the chippy and so they had to stand out on the street to wait. Jamie began a game of "guess the job" which involved matching each person in the shop with a job. The woman at the front of the queue, he decided, had to be a rat catcher because of her pointed nose and ferrety eyes. The fact that she had whiskers probably helped. The man behind her was most likely a beekeeper because of his red face and hands which had obviously been stung a lot. And the man with the shorts on showing off his hairy legs just had to be… His musings were interrupted by the arrival on top of the lamp post across the road of a large black-backed gull. Aimee was looking at the advertising cards in the window and hadn't seen it yet so he decided to keep her attention from it.

The rat catcher and the beekeeper both left at the same time and Jamie was able to bustle Aimee inside although it did involve nudging the old lady in front to get her to move along.

"When do you think it would be a good time to open the jar up, Sis? Do you think Mum would miss us if we went upstairs after tea? You could say that your head was aching and I could volunteer to look after you while she watched that hospital thing on telly."

Aimee looked quizzically at him. "Ok, what are you up to?" she asked, "There's something going on in that head of yours and I want to know what it is."

"Nothing, honestly, Aimee… I just want to see what's in the jar that's all. I want to know if everything went alright for him. I want…" As he spoke his eyes quickly, involuntarily looked out towards the lamp post. The gull was still there. "I want to…"

Aimee had seen the movement of his eyes and turned to look for herself. Jamie did the only thing he could to distract her in time, he trod down hard on her foot and then for good measure he stepped back and trod on the foot of the old lady.

"Owww! What did you do that for?" Aimee moaned.

"Owww! Look what you're doing you clumsy thing," complained the old lady.

"Sorry, sorry… it was an accident. Me and my big feet, I'm always treading on things. I even tread on my own feet sometimes, ha ha ha."

"You can tread on your own as much as you like lad, just keep away from mine," the old lady warned.

"Hairy legs" was served and on his way as Jamie sneaked another look out of the window. It was still there but at least the queue was going down and now they were getting near to the counter he could start to play the new food game he had invented when he was here on his own last week. That was certain to keep her occupied.

"Hey, Sis, supposing you were in charge of the chippy, what new things would you sell?"

"Like what?" she asked, he was worse than usual tonight.

"Well I'd start doing… fried worms in spicy batter or mouse burgers in curry sauce!"

"I think you're going doolally… Three lots of fish and chips and two large cartons of peas please."

As Aimee waited for the order he walked over to the door and looked for the gull, it was still there. There was only one thing left that he could think of. He walked across the road to the lamp post and began shinning his way up it towards the gull. As he reached half way the metal post began to sway and the gull started to cry its squawking cry and flew away over the roof tops.

A police car pulled up alongside the post at the same time as Aimee came out of the shop.

It was quite nice to get a lift home from the chip shop even if it was only just along the road, but the fish and chips were barely warm by the time they sat down to eat them. Aimee could only stand by and watch as Jamie tried his best to explain to Mum why the Police had found him half way up a lamp post that was still swaying from his gull scaring. He didn't mention the gull of course and trying to persuade the Police that he had spotted a rare clouded yellow butterfly at the top of the post and wanted to get a closer look just left them shaking their heads in disbelief as they walked back to the car.

The meal was eaten in silence and when it was over Mum delivered her judgement on Jamie and it was one that Aimee didn't want to hear at all.

"Congratulations, Jamie, of all the stupid things you've ever done this has to be the winner. It's lucky for you that those policemen had a sense of humour or you might have been in jail by now… but don't you think you've got away with it my lad. You are grounded until I think that you have grown enough sense cells in that head of yours to be allowed out amongst the rest of the human race again."

"Muuuum! It's the summer holidays. I need to be out getting fresh air and a sun tan. I need the exercise or my muscles will shrink. Aimee needs me to be by her side in case she goes dizzy again and falls over."

Aimee tried to help by chipping in with, "Couldn't he go out if I went with him and made sure he stayed by my side all the time?"

"And how are you going to do that then, get a dog collar and lead for him? Mum objected and then after a moments thought said, "That might be an idea though!"

"Muuuum, I'll be good. I'll be gooder than good. I'll… I'll…do all the washing up, the cleaning, the lawns, the cooking…"

"Not the cooking!" Mum butted in, "I don't think Aimee and I could cope with that, but if you do all the other things without moaning then I might, might mind you, change my mind a bit earlier than otherwise. But one more bit of idiotic behaviour and you'll be grounded for life, got it?"

"Yes, Mum."

"Well, there's the sink, you know where the washing up liquid is and just in case you've forgotten since your last wash the water comes out of the tap!" Mum reminded him. "Aimee and I are going into the lounge to watch some telly, so when you've finished a cup of tea would be nice."

It wasn't until 'City Hospital' came on that Aimee managed to excuse herself, telling Mum that she was tired after the walk on the beach and would like to go to her room to lie down and listen to the radio. Jamie was already upstairs but his reason was a more honest; "I'm going to my room to sulk."

She crept quietly up the stairs, put her head around Jamie's door and watched him pulling faces at himself in his dressing table mirror for a few moments before she whispered, "Are you going to come and see what the postman brought us then, Dogbreath?"

They sat cross-legged on Aimee's bed; Jamie watching as his sister carefully scraped the wax seal from the lid to open it. Suddenly she stopped and looked up at him with a troubled expression. "Why were you up that lamp post? It was that gull again wasn't it?"

Jamie thought about lying to her but he knew she could see right through him, she knew him too well. "Yes, sorry, Sis, it's still watching for you."

To his surprise she smiled a one hundred watt beam of a smile and before he could do anything about it she leant across and kissed him sloppily on his forehead.

"What the heck was that all about?" he complained and wiped his head with his hand.

"It's you; you know sometimes you're nearly the perfect brother. You did it so I wouldn't get upset again and even when you got into right bother over it, you still accepted the punishment rather than let it upset me."

"That's still no reason to floppin' well snog me! And anyway, why only nearly perfect?"

"Because you're still a smelly little oik!" she grinned and tipped the jar upside down and out dropped a roll of brown parchment with a piece of blue ribbon tied around it. She slid the ribbon off, gently eased the letter open and flattened it out on the bed. The writing was beautiful to look at but difficult to read and it took them a little while to get used to its squiggles and loops, but eventually they managed to make sense of it.

My trusted Aymy and Jaymy,

All went as planned and the deed is done. Martha is back where she belongs and I have used the power of the Star Fall to see Francis. He was in Venice with an old friend of mine but I did not let them see me as he must learn to be his own man and not think his father is watching over him.

I will now tell you how I dealt with Lord Larus and brought my Martha back to me. When he came back to see if I had the Star Fall's secrets for him I told him I had but required of him a letter allowing the free passage of Martha before I would give it to him. He only agreed when I showed him the round flask containing the liquid. He was so taken by its glowing colours that I thought he had gone into a trance. I told him I would tell how to gain its power only when he signed the letter. Once done and I had the means to Martha's freedom in my hands I told him he must drink the liquid and await its effect. I reasoned that what happened to my finger would happen to him also. Indeed within mere moments of his drinking it down he began to be eaten up by it. Before my eyes holes appeared in his body and they grew and ate away at him until with his last mortal breath he cried out, "I will have my revenge Thomas May, my soul will not rest until I have it. All the power shall be mine!" But fear not for as he spoke the last word only a shadow remained and that shadow took wing and flew away. I then used the letter to release my Martha and the power to take Larus' wife and children to another land lest they be set upon by his enemies now that he was gone.

I have hidden the bottle in one of my secret places below the ground but I know the power has passed on to you Aymy, use it wisely and for the good it can bring. Lord Larus would surely have had only evil intentions for it.

Take care my friends,

Thomas

They both sat in silence for several minutes, Jamie trying to imagine the liquid eating away at Larus from the inside, Aimee thinking about the shadow taking wing and flying away.

It was Aimee that broke the silence as she suddenly and determinedly said, "I've got to go back to him. I've got to know more about the shadow, it might have been Larus escaping… it might have been a gull taking wing! It might be the same one that is trying to get me! I have to go back now!

"But you can't, not at this time. It's nearly nine o'clock, it'll be dark soon!"

Before he could do anything about it Aimee had taken hold of the bottle and ordered, "Take me back to Thomas May's cottage, I want to see him!"

She stood at the end of the garden and stared at the cottage for a little while before starting to move towards it. She had taken only a few steps when a woman's scream made her stand still and stare at the door. The door flew open and out ran Martha, eyes wide in a terrified stare, her face contorted with fear. She ran passed Aimee with no sense that she was there and on through the gate to collapse and huddle behind the wall.

Aimee followed her and as she looked down into her frightened, sad brown eyes she felt suddenly that she knew her so well. A crash made her turn back towards the cottage and she saw Thomas through the open doorway. He was moving frantically around the room and trying to hit out at something that was attacking him. She moved closer and could just about make out a blur of a shadow moving through the air at Thomas. It repeatedly aimed itself at his head, whilst Thomas could only try his best to fend it off with flailing arms. One such attempt caught the oil lamp that hung from the low roof beam and sent it crashing to the floor in front of the fire. The oil spread out from the shattered lamp and made its way towards the fire.

Aimee could see what was going to happen and ran towards the door calling out to Thomas to warn him, "Thomas, Thomas… the lamp, the fire! Get out quick, please get out!"

The oil reached the glowing cinders under the metal grid that held back the fire and with a sudden gush of flame exploded. Aimee was knocked back by the wave of heat that came out of the door and by the time she had recovered herself and turned back towards the cottage it was a mass of flames. The wooden furniture, the dried herbs hanging from the wooden roof beams and the straw filled mattress on the bed splattered with oil from the fallen lamp were all hideously aflame and surrounding Thomas May.

From above the awful sounds of the burning cottage, Aimee heard two others that would stay with her always. The first was a loud groan and a final cry of, "Martha…" from Thomas. The second was that laughing screech that she knew and dreaded but this time the gull found a voice that called out to her, "May is gone… Now I am ready for you, Aimee Hawthorn!"

With a sudden explosion of smoke and sparks the roof collapsed in on the cottage and Aimee was enveloped in burning hot dust. She had just enough mind to call out, "I want to go home!" and fell onto the bedroom carpet, coughing and crying.

Jamie instinctively knelt down and put his arms around her, whispering," It's alright, it's alright. You're back home again now Aimee. I'm here for you. Calm down, I'll get you a drink of water."

As her sobs died away she lifted her head, thankful to see the familiar shapes of her own room and Jamie's concerned face looking down at her with a glass of water in his hand. She shakily got to her feet, sat on the bed and took the glass from Jamie and gulped it dry, the coolness soothing her smoke infested throat. Gradually, as she calmed down and began to piece together what she had witnessed ready to tell him all about it, something caught her eye that couldn't be right. She looked first at her hands, then at her t-shirt and jeans. Finally she stood up and went across to the dressing table mirror and stared at her reflection in it. There was no trace at all of dirt or soot or smoke any where on her! She was as she had been before she had gone back to the cottage.

"Jamie... I did go away didn't I?"

"Yes, you were gone for about ten minutes or so. Why, what happened to make you so upset?"

It was her turn to protect Jamie from the truth now; at least for tonight to let him get some sleep - she knew she wouldn't. "Oh just something that confused me a bit. I'll try to work it out and tell you all about it in the morning. I'm alright now thanks, but I am pretty tired. I think we should try and get some sleep. Goodnight, Dogbreath."

"If you're sure, Sis... Goodnight," he gave a little wave and smile and left.

Aimee got changed into her pyjamas, went to the bathroom to clean her teeth then returned to lie on top of her bed, to think over the things she had seen: Martha, Thomas May's death, the gull and, most strangely, nothing on her to show that she had been anywhere near a fire when she had returned. She heard Mum come up stairs and go to bed. She listened to the cars going by on the road outside. She heard the cat from up the road fighting over its territory with the one from down the road and next door's dog out for his final 'toilet' of the day letting both of them know that his garden belonged to him. But Martha's frightened face stayed in her mind until the very last moments before sleep took over. Martha reminded Aimee of her Mum, especially when she thought back to the time when Mum had to tell them that Dad had gone away. It was the same frightened sadness in her beautiful brown eyes.

Chapter 8

Brainfood

Morning came well before Aimee was ready for it. The sunlight streaming in through her bedroom window and the shrieks and cries of gulls adding to the noise of cars driving off on their various ways, roused her just enough to allow the events of the previous evening to take over her head again. She went over each piece of the scene as it happened, like the action replays on the sports programmes. Again she saw Martha's eyes, saw Thomas trying desperately to fend off the blurry shadow, saw the lamp fall and scatter its oil all around the room and the fire that destroyed the cottage and ended Thomas' life. She returned to the shadow and tried hard to make out what it could be. The cry of a morning gull right by her window focussed her mind and she knew exactly what it was, or rather who it was; the gull! The gull and Lord Larus were one and the same! But how could they be? The gull is now and Larus was then so how could they be the same person… thing?

Her thoughts were broken by the radio alarm in Mum's room declaring that, "It's a beautiful morning and this song should get you up with a smile… Wake me up before you go go, I'm not planning on going solo…"

She heard Mum groan and grumble, "Bog off, Wham!" as she hit the off button and then came the padding of her feet as she made her way to the bathroom.

"Mum always starts the day with a smile," Aimee chuckled and then swung her legs around and out of bed. "I'll make her a cup of tea."

She went down to the kitchen, filled the kettle, switched it on and got the teapot and mugs ready. When the tea was ready she filled the three mugs and took them upstairs, putting Mum's on her bedside table and calling through the half open bathroom door, "Mum, there's a cup of tea in your room for you."

Mum's reply was a mixture of, "Thanks, love" and the toilet flushing.

Getting into Jamie's room was a bit more difficult. The door opened a little way then jammed itself against something that Jamie had left lying around on the floor. She kicked the base of the door and shouted through the gap, "Get your smelly body out of bed and open this door; I've made you a cup of tea!"

His reply was the expected, "Uuuughhh... what... oh er right... thanks, Sis," The door opened to reveal Jamie blinking the sleep from his eyes and holding a pair of underpants in his right hand, "Sorry, Sis, they must have come off in the wrong direction. Thanks for the tea." He took the mug and the door closed again.

Aimee went back to her room with her tea and sat down on the edge of her bed. She thought again of Larus and the gull; how could they be the same? She decided that she would have to brave the black hole that was Jamie's room and go through everything with him in the hope that he could come up with some ideas.

She sipped her tea and listened to Mum settling down in her bed, she'd be back to sleep again in a couple of minutes. She finished her tea and quietly made her way back to Jamie's room. This time she got in more easily and crept over to Jamie, now soundly asleep again and making murmuring noises. For some reason he had his underpants on his head now. The mug of tea was stood untouched on the floor going cold. She gently took hold of his shoulder and shook him, but this had no effect so she tried tactic number two. She uncovered his feet and tickled them, but again apart from making him giggle, his sleep continued. Tactic number three was called for. She stood on the end of the bed, took hold of a foot in each hand and lifted him upside down and shook him whilst saying the magic words, "Wake up you little toe rag!"

This seemed to do the trick and Jamie opened his eyes and said, "Ok, I admit it, I'm awake. Now do you think you can put me down so that I can drink that lovely cup of tea without it going straight to my head?"

Aimee took the hint and dropped him. His head hit the bed and he timbered over to end up lying face down with his feet on the pillow and his head at Aimee's feet. He raised his head and looked up at her. "You really have got a strong grip haven't you? I hope you're waking me up before dawn on a Sunday morning for a good reason."

"It's not before dawn, it's ten past dawn, and yes it is important; I need to pick your brains before Mum comes back to life again."

"Couldn't you have made do with boiled egg and soldiers?"

"Come on, sit up, drink your cold tea and plug your brain in. I've got to tell you what happened last night and you've got to help me answer some questions." She went through the entire story trying hard to remember every detail. When she had finished she looked at Jamie and asked, "So why didn't I have any trace of the fire on me when I got back and is it possible that the shadow is really Larus and really the gull that's after me?"

"Mmm… the easy ones first eh? Well it could be that the fire and all the soot and ashes belong to the past and when you came back they had to stay there."

Aimee shook her head in amazement at her brothers reasoning. "That's brilliant, Jamie, and it even makes sense! Thomas said that we were like ghosts in the past."

"It's a pity though," Jamie moaned.

"What do you mean a pity?"

"Well it means we can't bring back things to sell in antique shops; we could have made a fortune!"

Aimee ignored his greed and turned her attention to the second problem. "What about Larus, the shadow and the gull then, Brainbox?"

Jamie put his head in his hands and thought for several minutes, occasionally lifting his head and nodding to himself as if going through things bit by bit in his mind. Eventually he looked up at Aimee and gave his conclusions; "Well… if you think back to when Thomas was telling us about how he decided to put the liquid into two bottles and he lost his finger in one."

"Yes, I remember… go on."

"Well he said that he tested the other bottle, Larus', with his quill pen. Supposing that the quill pen was made with a gull feather; it would have been a bit of gull that was dissolved into the liquid that Larus drank. Perhaps the shadow was the mixture of the Star Fall liquid, Larus and the gull and perhaps that shadow was able to travel through time as well. Or at least not die so it's still around today. And you said its last words to Thomas were; "My soul will not rest until I have revenge and all of the power!" I think we've got a big problem here, Aimee!"

Aimee stared out of the window, her face emotionless but pale as she took in the magnitude of Jamie's words. She was convinced he was right and she could also add one more layer to the story; "If Larus' soul was still around and could change into a gull, then was he also able to become human? Was he the Dr Gill… Dr Gull?"

"Who's, Dr Gull?" Jamie asked.

Aimee realised that she hadn't told him about the night visitor in the hospital and quickly went through it with him.

"Great, so now we've got Larus himself coming after you. I bet I can't get rid of him with an umbrella!"

They heard Mum going down the stairs and decided to get dressed, have some breakfast and meet up back in Aimee's room while Mum listened to 'The Archers' on the radio - it usually kept her out of their way for an hour or so on a Sunday morning.

When Aimee arrived in the kitchen Mum was in the middle of telling Jamie what high expectations she had of him in the coming weeks now that she was going back to work. How he had to grow up and make sure his sister kept her head out of the way of any more hard objects. How he was not to leave the house without Aimee and that if Aimee told him to do something he must do it without arguments.

"Does that mean if I tell him to put his head down the bog while I flush it, he has to?" Aimee asked as she sat down at the table.

"Of course it does, love; I mean we've got to make sure he has a wash sometimes haven't we? And cleaning the toilet is on the list of jobs I've given him," she replied with a wicked smile, "See, number 7, between tidying up his room and making sure the gerbils are cleaned out."

Jamie turned and stared at Aimee, "Whose side are you on then?"

"Oh I don't take sides… I take advantage!"

"Brilliant, four weeks of the summer holidays left and I get to be Aimee's little helper. Whatever happened to my human rights?"

Mum looked at Aimee, smiled and said, "You get them when you become human. Now, as it's the last day of my holiday, I think it would be nice if you two treated me and took me out for dinner. Nothing too expensive… the Red House Hotel will do. I'll ring and book a table while you do the washing up, Jamie."

"That's not fair. What about Aimee, what's she going to do?" Jamie complained while Aimee sipped her tea and grinned.

"She's going to go upstairs and raid her piggy bank… she's paying for dinner!"

Aimee's grin disappeared and it was Jamie's turn to smile. "Nice one, Mum!" he laughed and happily began to clear the table.

Once Mum had left the room Aimee went and stood by him at the sink and asked quietly, "The Red House Hotel, isn't that the place that George Walmsley owns?"

"Yes, why?"

"Well he lives in Scowcroft now and perhaps there's some connection between him and Larus."

"Like what… Do you think he lets Larus sleep in the cellars or something? Do you think he rents Scowcroft from Larus? Perhaps Larus takes over his son's body and that's why he's so slimy!"

Aimee frowned, "Alright, don't go on. It's just that… well I… I need to start finding some answers and… and…"

"And you've decided to clutch at straws. Look, Aimee, we've already found out quite a bit and I know you're scared but I think we have to try and think things out before you go jumping to conclusions and accusing someone just because his son is a squirt of pimple puss," Jamie replied, "And anyway I think I've thought out a few more things to work on. I'll go through them with you while Mums having her Archers fix. Now come on, give me a hand or two with the washing up."

It didn't take them long to finish off the dishes and they made their way upstairs to Aimee's bedroom, pausing outside the lounge door to make sure Mum was settled into her listening. They heard the familiar 'Dum de dum de dum de dum, dum de dum de da da' of the theme music and the voice of David Archer complaining about the state of the grazing in the lower pasture and knew that Mum wouldn't disturb them for a while.

They sat on the bed and Aimee listened while her brother went through all the evidence they had collected so far; Thomas's letter, mud and soot, Larus's threat, the gull, the hospital visit, the bottle and it's powers that only worked for Aimee. Then he asked Aimee; "Why do you think Larus didn't do anything to you in the hospital when he had the chance to?"

Aimee thought hard but couldn't come up with any answers so after a short silence Jamie told her his own theory. "Have you noticed that the only times that anything has actually happened to you have been when you've had the bottle with you?"

Aimee went over the incidents involving the gull and Dr. Gull in her mind and had to agree that Jamie was right. "So what does that mean?"

"Well I think that the soul of Larus, whether it's in gull form or Dr. Gull form doesn't have enough power to get you unless it's boosted by being close to the power of the Star Fall liquid in the bottle. Remember he told Thomas that he wanted, "All the power," when he was tricked by him. We have to make sure we're really careful when we use the bottle and that you're never on your own when you're with it."

Aimee agreed that what he said made sense but it still left lots of questions to be answered. "So you're saying that I'm perfectly safe if I go out without the bottle, but if I want to use it I must take you with me as a sort of bodyguard?"

"Mmm… I like that, me a bodyguard!"

"That is going to take a bit of getting used to. I mean, let's face it, you're not really that good at looking after your own body are you?" Aimee smirked. "But seriously, Jamie, how do we get rid of Larus? We can't spend the rest of our lives looking over our shoulders every time we go out. We've got to do something about him haven't we?"

"Yes we have, but I think we'll have to work on that one," Jamie agreed with a worried look that didn't give Aimee any confidence that they might find the answer very easily if at all.

From downstairs they heard the 'Dum de dum' music again and knew it was the end of their free time. This was confirmed when Mum shouted up the stairs, "Right you two get yourselves cleaned, polished and presentable; we're due at the Red House in one hour."

Jamie actually cleaned up quite nicely and in his best white shirt and dark blue trousers looked pretty smart. Aimee also did her Mum proud and wore her beige cropped trousers with a dark green blouse. Mum was really pleased with the effort they had made and as they sat down at their table she said, "Well you two look great for my surprise birthday treat!"

Aimee and Jamie looked at each other in panic; neither had remembered to buy her even a card never mind a present.

Aimee thought fast; today was the twenty third of July - Mum's birthday was the seventh of October she was sure. "Mum, it's not your birthday today."

"I know love… that's the surprise," and she smiled, put her right hand in the air and clicked her fingers, "Garkon!"

The waiters were leaning lazily against the wall by the door that led to the kitchens. They looked at each other and the younger of the two was pressed into action by the other to attend to them.

"Good afternoon, what can I get for you, Ladies, Gentleman?"

"Ooh, isn't he the posh one?" Mum chuckled, "Have you decided what you want yet, Aimee?"

"I'll have prawn cocktail please."

"Jamie?"

"I'll have the soup of the day."

Mum raised her eyebrows at him.

"Er... Please," he corrected himself.

"And I'll have the smoked salmon roulade please." Mum completed the orders by deciding, "And we'll all have the roast beef."

"Thank you, Madame," and off he scuttled to the kitchens, rolling his eyes at the other waiter on the way.

The other waiter suddenly burst into action as he saw a large black car stop outside the door. He rushed to open the door and bowed as the occupants came in. The other diners, the Hawthorns included, all turned and craned their necks to see who the new customer was. They must be pretty famous to get such attention they assumed. One or two did recognise George Walmsley and settled back in their seats, but most had no idea who he was.

Aimee and Jamie both knew, not because they recognised him, but because they recognised the slimy oik of a boy who followed his parents in. Jamie slipped a little lower in his seat in the hope that Jordon would not spot him. Aimee on the other hand looked straight at him and even smiled and winked when he looked in her direction. She was certain that he would be too embarrassed about what had happened at school to cause a fuss as any boy would be.

But she didn't realise just how much of a slime ball Jordon Walmsley really was.

The memory of being shown up in front of his cronies brought with it the feelings of anger and yearning for revenge that he had stored up inside him. He pulled on his father's sleeve and when he turned around whispered something in his ear that turned his face a deep shade of red.

The waiter returned from the kitchen carrying the starters. As he approached the table George Walmsley moved to stand in his path and with the merest movement of his eyes sent him on his way back to the kitchen.

Walmsley then turned and spoke to Mum in a voice that was treacly smooth but loud enough for the whole room to hear. "My son tells me that your daughter has been bullying him at school. He tells me that he wouldn't have worried me with it but he didn't think he could eat his Sunday lunch knowing that she was here staring at him in a threatening way across the room. I know that my son is capable of looking after himself, but your daughter is obviously a lot older and bigger than he is and with her threatening to get her gang on to him I thought it best to intervene. I think it might be for the best if you left my restaurant now and saved my little Jordon any more upset."

Jordon smirked and, unable to resist called out, "Yeh, go on, get out, Aimee Hawthorn and take your stupid little brother with you. I'm going to eat before you today, ha ha ha!"

Mum matched Walmsley for shades of red with her embarrassment and anger. "How could Aimee do this to her... Aimee not Jamie," she thought, it was hard for her to take it in. But worse was to come.

As they stood up to leave Walmsley spoke again, "Hawthorn? Did you say their name was Hawthorn, Jordon?

"Yes, Dad, Aimee and Jamie Hawthorn," he sing-songed their names mockingly.

"And would you be related to Mike Hawthorn by any chance?" he asked, looking at all three of them as if they were criminals.

It was Mum that answered; her embarrassment was now turning into defensive anger. "He is my husband, their father and what of it?"

"Seen him lately have you, only he owes me a lot of money?"

The room around them was completely silent, all eating had stopped, and everyone was watching and listening to this great soap opera-like entertainment. Even the usual sounds of cooking and clattering of dishes from the kitchen had stopped as waiters, chefs, and washers-up left their work to gather round the kitchen door to take in the drama.

"I haven't seen Mike for five years now and if you're the one that chased him away then I think you ought to know that when he gets back he'll sort you out. He's got evidence that will send you to prison for a very long time whoever you are!"

Aimee looked at her Mum with astonishment. Did she know more than was in that torn up letter? Had Dad been in touch with her again since he went away? Where was he now; did she know?

Jamie just looked at Mum's red and angry face and wondered what on earth she was on about? What was Walmsley on about? When and where and what were they going to eat?

"I know he's got nothing on me and I want my money. If you happen to hear from him again you let him know I still remember him and I look forward to meeting him again," Walmsley finished with a sneer and walked over to where his well decorated wife sat with the still sneering Jordon.

Mum pushed Aimee and Jamie out of the restaurant and down the road towards the seafront. When they reached the sea wall she slumped down on a bench and burst into tears.

Aimee sat next to her, put her arm around her shoulder and hugged her saying repeatedly," It's all right, Mum, it's all right."

Jamie stood at their side and after a few minutes, when Mum seemed to be calming a little, he suggested, "If I go and fetch a pizza from Guiseppi's can we go home and eat and can you explain what that was all about because I'm starving and very confused in that order."

Aimee looked up at him and shook her head, "Jamie, stop thinking about yourself will you!"

"No, love, it's alright. I think it's about time you both knew about why your father left us. You're both big enough and old enough now and I know how well you look after each other so I think you'll cope. And as for the pizza... I could murder one. Here," she said, taking a twenty pound note from her purse, "Go and fetch a selection of whatever you want, both of you, I'll meet you back up at the house."

They separated and Mum walked back up the hill towards home while Aimee and Jamie walked along the seafront to Guiseppi's.

"Don't look now but I think your gull is watching us!" Jamie warned as they entered the pizza house.

"Right at this moment I don't give a stuff about Larus or the gull or whatever. All I'm bothered about is Mum and Dad and us."

"And the pizzas... what shall we have? I fancy the "Spicy Meat Feast Special" with extra topping and some of that "Triple Whipple Choco-fudge" ice cream for afters."

Aimee smiled, "You have that, Jamie... you have that. Now what would Mum like do you think? Let's not skimp, I've brought my piggy money so let's enjoy ourselves before Mum spills the beans about Dad eh?"

Mum had washed her face and removed the smeared mascara by the time they arrived home with the feast and she looked a lot better, which helped to cheer everyone up. The well chosen and ample pizzas followed by the wide selection of ice creams - Jamie couldn't make up his mind so got some of everything - also helped to raise the mood, so that by late afternoon they all were quite jolly.

But Jamie had not forgotten Mum's promise to reveal all about Dad and as soon as they settled down after clearing the table he said to her, "Right, now what have you got to tell us about Dad then?"

Mum sat forward in her chair and nervously rubbed the back of her left hand with her right hand for a few moments before she'd composed herself enough to speak. She turned her wedding ring round and round on her finger as she looked at her children and began.

"Your Dad left us all five years ago because he got himself into debt trying to look after the men who worked for him on the boat. The fish catch had been poor and he had to borrow money to keep the boat and crew going… only when the bank refused to lend him any more it seems he went to George Walmsley for a loan. Well things didn't get any better and Walmsley took over ownership of the boat and then started asking your Dad to do things that he knew were wrong."

"Like what, Mum?" Jamie asked.

"I suppose you're both old enough to know now," Mum paused to gather her thoughts. Aimee blushed and looked down at the floor; she knew what Mum was going to tell them already from reading Dad's letter.

"Was it illegal stuff?" Jamie pressed.

"Yes it was, Jamie, but your Dad wouldn't do it. Walmsley wanted your Dad to sail to the Continent and bring back things that he wasn't allowed to bring back," She continued, finding it hard to come up with the best way of explaining.

Aimee could see how upset it was making her having to go over events that had caused her so much anguish. She decided to help her even though she might find out about the letter. "Walmsley wanted him to smuggle drugs and people into the country didn't he?"

Mum looked at her and realised that she knew a lot more than she should.

Aimee looked at Mum and nodded to let her know she was right.

"So why didn't Dad go to the police? He could have got Walmsley locked up," Jamie asked; he was getting more and more angry knowing that the slimeball's Dad had been the cause of his own Dad going away.

"Because Walmsley would have denied it and besides your Dad still owed him a lot of money and he would have got his "friends" to sort him out. In fact that's what he tried to do and that's why your Dad went away. He wanted to get the money together to pay off Walmsley and also try to keep him from making our lives a misery. He managed to keep us out of it... until today that is. You see I didn't know it was George Walmsley that he was running from until he spoke to us like that in the restaurant. Now I don't know what will happen," She closed her eyes and slumped back into her chair, her head lolling forward, her chin resting on her chest.

After letting Mum recover a little Aimee asked the question she had wanted to ask every time she thought about her Dad; "Mum, has Dad been in touch with you since he went away, since he left us those letters?"

Mum remained in the same position for a few moments then opened her eyes and looked first at Aimee then at Jamie before closing them again. Then suddenly she sat upright opened her eyes and began. "Aimee, Jamie... you know that it was your Dad's idea to give you those names. That is we both liked Aimee for a name. There was a girl called Aimee who came to our school, she'd had a rotten time of it. Her Dad hit her Mum and got sent to jail and her Mum got drunk every night so that Aimee got put into care. We both felt proper sorry for her but she was sent to live somewhere down south just when we were getting to know her. When we got married and you came along we both wanted to name you after her and hoped we could do a better job of looking after you. And then when you came along, she smiled at Jamie, your Dad came into the hospital all smiles and announced that you must be called Jamie because he'd had a dream and an old man had been sort of singing, 'Aimee Jamie, watch them grow, Aimee Jamie, watch them go.' Your Dad was daft like that you know."

Aimee and Jamie looked at each other and, thinking of Thomas, they smiled.

"He'd do things on a whim, on the spur of the moment. At least to others it seemed like that, but I knew he always thought hard about the things he did before he did them. That's why I trusted him so much and that's why I knew that if he said he had to go away to sort things out then that is what he had to do. Yes I have heard from him once or twice. I had a phone call from France about six months after he left just to say he was alright and to ask about how we were getting along. He said he couldn't stay on the line for long in case they were tapping our phone. Then about a year after that I had a letter from Italy saying he was doing alright helping out on a fishing boat in the Mediterranean Sea and had managed to save quite a bit of money up. I had a few other letters from there saying more or less the same and then I got one that said he was hoping to come home soon. That was two years ago and I haven't had any since. I was so excited but as the weeks and months passed and he didn't turn up I'm afraid I started to lose hope. I thought that the ones who were after him must have found him and…" She stopped herself saying what she thought but couldn't stop herself from crying and anyway both Aimee and Jamie knew exactly what she was going to say.

"But Walmsley is still looking for him," Jamie exclaimed, "He as good as said so. He said he was looking forward to meeting him again to get his money back!"

"Jamie's right, Mum, he did say that!" Aimee added encouragingly.

This revelation had little effect on Mum as she continued to sob whilst glugging out the question; "Then… where is… he?"

Aimee made an instant, Dad-like decision, "I don't know, but I promise you we…" and she took hold of Jamie's hand, "are going to find him and bring him back to you."

Mum stopped crying, wiped a sleeve across her eyes and in a voice that was stern and deeply serious said, "I don't want either of you getting mixed up in this, I couldn't bear anything to happen to you as well. Keep away from Walmsley… keep out of it please. You must promise me that you will not interfere!"

"But, Mum, we want our Dad back and anyway Aimee can… Ow!" Jamie let out a yelp as Aimee bent back the fingers on the hand she still held.

"Aimee can what? She's a young teenage girl and you're her little brother. Just what chance do you think you stand against them and their money… and their connections? They've probably got contacts all over the place, thieves, murderers, probably even in the police! Look, I know you mean well but if your Dad couldn't sort it, then what chance have you got? Now promise me that you won't go near George Walmsley."

They both looked into their Mum's blood-shot eyes and nodded. She widened her eyes and cocked her head to one side and Aimee knew she wanted more than a nod.

"We…" she squeezed Jamie's hand.

"We promise," they both agreed.

"Good, now if you two don't mind I'm going to go up and have a little lie down, I've got a lot to think about and some peace and quiet in a darkened room might help. You two see if you can keep yourselves quietly occupied for a couple of hours or so."

They waited until they heard the floorboards above them creak and the sound of the curtains being drawn before they turned towards each other to speak.

Aimee had already decided the first step but it was Jamie that said it first, "Right, I suggest the first thing we have to do is find Dad."

Aimee smiled as once again the great minds had thought alike, but she then had another thought - what if Dad was dead? She didn't say so to Jamie but the thought had been lingering around in her mind since Mum had said she hadn't heard from him since he'd written that he was hoping to come home soon two years ago and then not written again. She was shocked though when Jamie went on, "If he's still alive that is."

"Jamie! How can you think like that? Of course he's still alive... I'm sure he is...he must be for Mum's sake," she tried to convince herself as much as Jamie.

"I'm sure you're right, Sis, but I think we have to be prepared for anything and one thing's for sure; no matter what, we are going to get even with Walmsley for him!"

"Agreed!" Aimee concurred. "Mum's back at work tomorrow so we'll start our investigations then. I'll use the bottle to find Dad while you have a wander around the harbour and see if you can find out who is working on the Dancing Sally now. We might be able to find out what Walmsley's up to by being around them."

"But not by going anywhere near Walmsley," Jamie smirked, "Hey, you're getting as sneaky as I am, Sis!"

"Oh, I'm not as daft as you look. Turn the telly on and we'll watch that police thing to see if it gives us any ideas."

"Oh yes, 'Inspector Bottom,' I like that," he grinned.

Chapter 9

Dad

Aimee was the first to wake up next morning. She looked at the clock on her bedside table and was surprised to see that it was nearly half past nine. "Strange that Mum didn't wake me up before she went to work, she usually gives us the "no fooling around" warning," she murmured to herself as she threw back the duvet and swung her feet out and onto the floor.

She gave her eyes a rub and went over to the window to have her look out at the weather that she had every morning. It was a bright, blue sky day with just the odd cloud or two wandering across the sky on their way out to sea. There was no sign of the gull, but then she was becoming almost used to it now so that, although she was still fearful, she managed to keep a level head. It hadn't found a way of getting to her in the house yet and Jamie seemed to be pretty good at fending it off outside.

She made her way out of her room and along to Mum's where she found her muttering and making little snorting noises but obviously still very asleep. She put her hand on Mum's left shoulder and shook her firmly to which Mum responded by swinging her right arm over and nearly catching her with a smack on her head. Luckily the action served to wake her and she looked up at Aimee with blinking eyes.

"What... what's the matter? What time is it? Why are you shaking me?"

Aimee smiled then quietly explained, "Its half past nine, you've forgotten to put your alarm on and you're late for work, Mum."

"Half past nine!" Her eyes widened, she sat up and panic set in. "I... er, I'm late, I should be there by now... they'll give me the sack... then what will we do with no money? We'll... we'll..."

"We'll get you up and ready, we'll get a quick breakfast ready for you, we'll get you off to work and while you're on your way we'll ring them and tell them that the car wouldn't start and you had to wait until Mr Howard next door started it with his jump leads…Ok?" Aimee nodded.

Mum nodded back and smiled, "You're getting too good at making things up young lady."

"And you're getting too good at staying in bed, Mum, get going will you!"

Aimee went quickly along the landing and hammered on Jamie's door shouting, "Downstairs now, Jamie, Mum's late and we've got to help her get going!" Then she went down to the kitchen, put the kettle on, put some bread in the toaster, got the cups, teapot and plates ready and took the butter from the fridge.

Jamie arrived just as the toast popped up and without pausing he grabbed it, put it on a plate and began to butter it.

The kettle boiled and Aimee poured the water into the waiting teapot and took it to the table.

Jamie returned to the toaster and reloaded it.

Aimee spread some marmalade on the toast and cut the slices into triangles.

Mum arrived. Washed, dressed and made up she set about demolishing the toast and tea.

As Aimee and Jamie sat down to their breakfast so Mum stood up, gave each of them a kiss on the forehead and with a parting reminder about fooling around, left.

They heard the car start first time and squeal off the driveway and Aimee took the phone off its wall holder and pressed the preset to call Sudworth's.

"Hello, Sudworth Printers, how can I help you?"

"Hello, Angie, it's Aimee, Mum's going to be a bit late I'm afraid… the alarm didn't go off. It's my fault really cos' Mum's been worrying about me too much."

"Oh I see… 'the car wouldn't start.' I'll make sure Mr Sudworth gets the message, don't worry. And how are you feeling, Aimee, it sounded really nasty?"

"I'm not too bad now, the stitches have nearly dissolved and the scar isn't too obvious if I keep my hair brushed across it. Thanks for Mum, Angie. I think she needs a bit of looking after herself now she's sorted me out."

"No problem… ah here's Mr Sudworth now, I'll pop and soften him up for when Sally gets here. He's a sweetie really you know. Bye."

"Bye." Aimee put the phone back and they finished their toast in silence, except for Jamie's noisy slurps as he drank his tea. They put their empty cups down at the same time, looked at each other, nodded and together rose from the table and rushed up to Aimee's room to make their plans for the day.

"Right, I'm going to get dressed and then I'm going to ask the bottle to take me to Dad and if I can, I'll get him to come home," Aimee decided.

"But how are you going to do that? You can't just appear in front of him and say, "Hi, Dad it's me, Aimee I've come to take you home with this magic bottle!" He won't recognise you for a start and he'll probably think you're a head case if you try and explain all that's happened to you with Thomas and Larus and the gull… And what about the gull, it might follow you and be there waiting for you!" Jamie objected.

"I've thought through all that and I think I've come up with some answers. I'll go to Dad a few seconds behind the present time and that way no one else will see me and he will only see a blurry shape at most, just like Thomas said he saw us. If I'm careful he won't be aware that I'm there at all. I can see that he's alright, find out where he's living and then come back here and write to him and tell him to come home when we've sorted Walmsley out. As for Larus, well he's never bothered me when I've been in the past so with a bit of luck either he can't follow me there or at least he can't see or touch me if he is there. Perhaps that's why he wants the rest of the power, so he can travel. It's a chance I'll have to take." Aimee said decisively.

Jamie saw the logic of what she was saying and couldn't see any reason to argue with it despite his worries. "Ok, but take care and use the bottle to come back if there's even the slightest hint of a problem. I'll pop down to the harbour and see what I can find out about the 'Sally' and her crew. I know the bloke who works on the ice cream van down there, he might be able to let me know a few things if I ask him."

"Hey, don't just go up to him and say, "Have you seen any dodgy goings on around that boat over there?" You never know he might be one of Walmsley's cronies as well." Aimee warned.

"Don't worry, Sis; I've seen enough cop shows to know how to go about it. I'll act dumb and just ask general things like, "That's a nice boat, where does it do its fishing?" And, "By heck, he looks a rough bloke, what's his name? I want to stay clear of him if I can." That way I'll get into conversation without him realising I'm pumping him for information!" Jamie smiled at his own cleverness.

"Pumping him for information?" Aimee scowled, "Where did you get that from?"

Jamie grinned, again ever so pleased with himself, "Micky Scott said it in 'Crime City Casebook' last week. Mind you he ended up being caught by the gang and being badly beaten up - but he was alright again for this weeks episode."

"Yes, well you just watch out, this gang might not beat you up badly, they might be good at it!"

"Nice one, Sis! I'll get out of these piggy jam jams and into my working clothes then I'll get you the bottle from my super secret hiding place."

"You just get yourself ready and I'll get the bottle from behind the hot water tank in the airing cupboard."

"How did you know it was there?" Jamie asked, astounded that she knew one of his best hiding places.

Aimee winked at him and said, "I've told you before, I'm not as daft as you look!"

By the time she had retrieved the bottle Jamie was back in her room ready and waiting to see her. "I've had a look out of the window and the gull is on the shed roof. I'll go down and keep it occupied while you get dressed and do your disappearing act, ok?"

"Thanks, Bruth, see you later... and remember; take care!"

"Snap, Sis," he replied with a click of his fingers and set off down the stairs and out into the back garden.

Aimee watched from behind closed curtains and couldn't help laughing and yet admiring his ingenuity. First he walked nonchalantly down the path towards Mum's vegetable patch, being careful not to even glance up at the gull. Then he bent over and untied one end of the netting that held up the runner beans, tip-toed along the patch and untied the other end. He collected the netting together in a neat, well folded bundle and with his back to the gull, which was watching him closely after its previous forays with him, he tied some fist-sized stones to the corners. In a split second he whirled around and threw the bundle up in the air and over the gull trapping it in the netting on top of the shed.

The gull screeched and tried to take flight and at first the netting tangled around its wings but then, almost without pausing, it lifted its head and tore the netting to shreds with it's razor sharp beak and was away.

Holding the bottle tightly in her left hand, Aimee closed her eyes and thought carefully before taking a deep breath and asking the bottle to; "Take me to where my Dad was ten seconds ago please."

Even before she opened her eyes she felt as if she knew where she was. There was that smell and sound that only hospitals seem to have. To this was added the regular beeping sound of a heart monitor that she recognised from the many hospital dramas she had watched with Mum.

She opened her eyes and found she was in the corner of a small room with white, windowless walls and a tiled floor. In the centre of the room, with its headboard to the wall opposite the door, was a hospital bed with the heart monitor and a stand holding a drip bottle at the side. In the bed with his face towards the ceiling and eyes peacefully shut was Dad. His hair was longer and greyer than she remembered and his face was older with a thin scar across his forehead above his left eye. But it was definitely Dad.

As she stood at the end of the bed and gazed down on the prone figure of her Dad her eyes welled up and she burst into great gulping sobs of tears. It was a mixture of happiness and relief... he was alive! The sight of him lying in a hospital bed wired up to a heart monitor and feeding tubes was a small matter, he was alive and she had found him.

When her tears had stopped she went around to the side of the bed and began talking quietly to him, telling him about how much she and

105

Mum and Jamie were missing him. She told him about Walmsley and his weasely son and the restaurant. She was still talking an hour later when the door suddenly opened and she turned to see who had entered. It was a nurse followed by what she supposed was a doctor in a white gown and someone in a smart grey suit.

The nurse went over to Dad, lifted his head gently and adjusted his pillow. She then opened his mouth a little and, with what looked like a baby's drinking bottle, tipped a small amount of liquid into it before letting his head rest back on the pillow. She then wiped his lips with some of the liquid to moisten them and stood back to check the drip bottle.

Aimee was a little surprised that Dad hadn't woken up but she stood to one side as the doctor picked up Dad's chart from the end of the bed and began to look at the graphs and notes. She moved beside him and looked at the charts herself. They were very similar to the ones she'd had in hospital a few weeks ago but there was one very obvious difference; the writing on these charts was not in English, it was Italian. Dad was in an Italian hospital. She could make out one or two words having done a "taster" course at school before she decided to take French and Spanish. Oh how she wished she'd chosen Italian!

The doctor looked towards Dad's face and commented, "I see there has been little change in his condition, Nurse Pellegrini."

"No, Doctor Di Piedi, I'm afraid not."

"And our fine Inspector here has had no luck in finding out who he is?"

The man in the grey suit reddened a little then smiled at the nurse and added, "No, I am afraid he is still a mystery to us. We have circulated his picture throughout Italy and Interpol have contacted police forces all over Europe and America without success. You would think that after two years someone would be missing him and come forward. If only there had been some documents on him when he was found, but whoever did him over left us with nothing to go on. I suppose we'll have to wait until he wakes up to make any progress."

"You do realise that even if he does come out of the coma he may have memory loss," Doctor Di Piedi warned.

"Yes, I understand. Is there any way that you can jog him out of it?"

"No, not really… Sometimes a familiar voice has some effect but that is of little use in his case as we don't even know who he is or where he comes from. I am afraid you will just have to keep on looking Inspector and we will have to keep on hoping," the Doctor replied with a shake of his head.

The two men left the room and as Nurse Pellegrini continued to check all the tubes and wires she spoke softly to Dad. "Well, Mr Mystery, another beautiful day slipping away and no nearer to solving the puzzle. It's such a shame; you really are quite a handsome man. Well at least you would be if ever the sun could get to you. And look at the effect you're having on me! I'm chatting you up and I don't know if you understand what I'm saying even if you can hear me. Ah well, I don't suppose you mind do you?"

It was only at that point that it suddenly dawned upon Aimee that she had understood every word that had been spoken. "But… if this is Italy, why aren't they speaking Italian?" she thought and frowned in puzzlement.

As the nurse spoke again Aimee looked at her and noticed something that she had not noticed before. Her lips seemed to be saying something different to what she was hearing. She had picked up the chart and was speaking as she wrote on it. "Temperature… thirty seven degrees… fluid intake one point four litres."

Aimee looked over her shoulder at the chart; she had written in Italian but spoken in English! "I wonder…" She thought and put the bottle down on the bed.

As the nurse replaced the chart and turned to leave she called out cheerily, "Buona giornata!"

"The bottle must translate for me… Brilliant! Now I think I'll get back and see how Jamie has got on." She picked up the bottle, walked around the bed to Dad's head, leaned over him and kissed him on the forehead, "Bye for now Dad, I'll be back to take you home soon I promise. Take me home now please…"

As Aimee vanished a flicker of a smile formed on Mike Hawthorn's lips.

A very big smile was on Aimee's face as she reappeared back in her bedroom, she couldn't wait to tell Jamie that she had found Dad and that he wasn't dead. She stood still where she had arrived back, facing the bedroom curtains, and let the memory of her Dad lying peacefully in the Italian hospital bed drift around in her mind.

"So you've returned to me at last, Aimee Hawthorn!"

Aimee, startled out of her reminiscences, turned around and faced Lord Larus. She gripped the bottle tightly in her right hand and quickly put it behind her back.

"I've been waiting a long time to meet you again and I see you have my Star Fall with you… very good. I'd like it back now if you don't mind young lady. I have plans for it." Larus' voice was chillingly smooth and deep.

Her right hand started to move around to the side of her body without her intending it to. She couldn't decide whether it was doing it on its own or perhaps Larus was making it move. What she could decide was that she couldn't stop it moving so she had to the only thing she could think of; she leapt up onto her bed to her right and with one great bounce landed on the other side of it and made for the door.

Larus turned and lurched forward to make a grab for her but managed only to grasp a few strands of her hair which came away in his hand.

Aimee felt the sharp pain on her scalp but carried on through the door, catching hold of it and slamming it shut behind her. As she reached the top of the stairs she turned and caught a glimpse of Larus opening the door and striding out onto the landing. She didn't linger to think about what had happened but took the stairs several at a time and in four jumps landed in the hallway. The front door opened as she landed and in walked Jamie.

Seeing Aimee land with such force startled him but he had no time to say anything as she shouted, "Larus!" at him and turned to look up at the looming figure on the staircase.

Jamie looked up at him and without pausing to think he moved forward to the bottom of the stairs to block his way. He did have to think though as a quivering oily coldness moved through him and left in its wake the worst feeling of wanting to be sick that he had ever felt. His eyes went blurred and so did his head but he managed to turn and as they cleared he saw that Larus was moving towards Aimee who was cornered with her back to the kitchen door.

"Aimee… PASS!" he shouted and Aimee immediately threw the bottle over Larus. Jamie caught it in both hands and turned to run up the stairs.

Larus wheeled around and dived after him and with his right hand caught hold of his left foot. He gripped tightly - now that Jamie held the bottle he was solid to him and he pulled him back down the stairs. Jamie kicked out with his right foot and managed to hit Larus on the chest but this only seemed to make his grip grow stronger and his lips creased upwards at the edges to form a smile so ugly that Jamie squealed with fear.

"Jamie… PASS!" Came the call from Aimee and again the bottle flew through the air. It scraped the hall ceiling but with a stretch she caught it and opened the kitchen door.

As soon as the bottle left Jamie's hand Larus' hand passed through his foot and he was free to scuttle up the stairs to his bedroom and away from him.

Larus stood up and shouted angrily, "I grow angry at these games. I will have the power of the Star Fall and if I have to destroy this house and you to get it… then so be it!"

Aimee walked slowly out of the kitchen holding the bottle above her head, "Do you really think that we will allow you to have all the power that this gives? You… you killed Thomas May and you've probably killed lots of other people!"

"Lots? I would say hundreds, maybe thousands… one loses count of such trivialities. Now give me the power before I add one more to the count." Larus inclined his head slightly and held out his hands.

"Oh, I don't think so. What's to stop you killing us even if I do hand it over?" She paused as she saw Jamie creep around the bottom of the stairs with one hand behind his back. "I mean, you've got to give us something in return… our freedom and safety at least."

"You may have that, you mean nothing to me. You are merely an irritation, a pimple on the face of a mighty Lord… Lord Larus, master of time!" Larus sneered. "Oh, and I know that your pea brain of a brother is behind me! But what can he do? Ha! He is not even a pimple!"

Jamie smiled at his sister and nodded.

Aimee looked into Larus' eyes and said in a calm, firm voice, "Our freedom and safety then… Shake hands on it." She held out her right hand and as Larus took hold of it she squeezed it tightly and felt the cold grip of her enemy squeeze back.

"You have a good grip, Aimee Hawthorn and you have been a good adversary. I…" He had no chance to finish his triumphal speech as the cricket bat thudded into his skull and he dropped to the floor.

"Oh well played, sir, a six I think!" Aimee smiled.

Jamie held the bat up in the air and smiled back, "So do you think I'll make the team next…"

His banter was cut short by the sight of Larus' body shrinking and fading into a shadow that rose up from the floor, drifted around their heads and then at some speed flew straight through the kitchen window. The window bulged outwards as the shadow went through, then returned to its normal flatness and promptly shattered into tiny pieces - just as Mum walked in through the front door.

"Aimee, Jamie… I thought I'd pop home for lunch to see how you're behaving… What the hell have you been playing at?"

Jamie looked at the widow, then at his cricket bat, then at Aimee, shrugged his shoulders and said with a pleading puppy smile, "Cricket?"

Aimee began to say, "It wasn't his fault," but Mum beat her to it.

"I hold you responsible for this, Aimee Hawthorn! You were supposed to be watching out for him while he was grounded. You are the older one… and he couldn't play cricket on his own now could he? Someone had to bowl didn't they? So it's you that's going to pay for that window. I'll ring a glazier, you start clearing the glass from out of the sink. And, Jamie, make me a cup of tea. Now!" Mum ordered then went to the lounge to look in the phone book for the number.

"Well, I think we got away with that one quite lightly!" Jamie smiled.

"We… I've got to clean this up and pay for it! That Larus is getting to be a proper nuisance." Aimee moaned.

"What do you mean getting to be? We've got rid of him haven't we?"

"Got rid of him? I should think we've only made him madder. He'll be back, you watch, he'll be back!"

Chapter 10

Dadnap!

Miraculously the glazier arrived to look at the window just as Mrs Hawthorn was setting off back to work. He'd been on a job just around the corner and popped in to take the measurements during his break. Apparently the window was a standard sized double glazed unit and he could pick a replacement up and have it fitted by the end of the day and all for one hundred and thirty pounds.

"One hundred and thirty pounds!" moaned Aimee, "That's my piggy empty and on a diet for the next hundred years!"

"Yes, but look on the bright side… you won't get zits from eating too much chocolate because you won't be able to buy any," Jamie sniggered.

"Thanks a lot, Dogbreath, but remember," she lowered her voice and feigned an evil whisper, "I am still your prison guard and you don't go anywhere without my permission."

"And I don't suppose you'll let me forget it," he complained.

"You bet I won't. Now let's see, it's two o'clock and the glass man is supposed to be coming back about four-ish so that gives us two hours to sort ourselves out. How did you get on this morning? Did you find out anything useful down at the docks?"

Jamie smiled, held his head up, closed his eyes and said proudly, "Your super sleuth of a brother only managed to get the names of every one of the crew of the Dancing Sally. And what's more," here his tone changed to one of anger, "that creep, Walmsley still has the boat registered in Dad's name!"

"But Dad said that he'd had to sign it over to Walmsley so why would he leave it registered in Dad's name? ...Unless... unless he wanted..." Aimee paused, thinking that not even George Walmsley could be so conniving and evil. It was Jamie that completed her theory.

"Unless he wanted Dad to take all the blame if anything went wrong."

"He couldn't be that vindictive could he?" Aimee asked, looking at her brother with a worried frown.

"From what I found out this morning...yes. I talked to an old mate of Dad's, Billy Mackie. He used to work on the boat with him before he retired and he does some volunteer work at the Seaman's Mission now. I saw him standing outside it and when I asked about the Dancing Sally he told me some right stories about Dad." Jamie grinned and shook his head as he recalled some of them, "And he told me that when the Sally comes back to port Walmsley is always there and he always has a big bust up with the skipper, Davy Loughlain. He gave me the names of the crew, the regulars anyway; he said that sometimes he sees other men on the boat that he doesn't recognise."

"I bet they're the ones that Walmsley's smuggling in from the continent," Aimee decided, "Did Billy mention anything about packages?"

"No, sorry, Sis, I forgot to ask about that. But it was Billy who told me about the registration, he was surprised as well because he hadn't seen Dad around for so long. He asked me about him and I told him that he'd had to go to look after his sick auntie in Sheffield."

"Sheffield, Why Sheffield?"

"Because it was the first place that came into my head... Sheffield Wednesday are called Wednesday because a cricket team used to keep fit in the winter by playing football on Wednesdays and they got known as the Wednesday Football Club. And they're called the

'Owls' because they used to play at Owlerton." he rattled off the facts like a talking computer.

"Thank you, Mr Encyclopaedia," Aimee said sarcastically, "And now back to the important stuff. I think that we should try and be at the docks when the Sally comes back from its next trip. See if you can find out when that will be."

"It leaves tomorrow morning at high tide, about five o'clock, and it should be back on Friday evening," he replied smugly.

"Well done, Bruth… er, just one other thing. I thought you said you would get your info from the ice cream man."

Jamie's face clouded a little as he thought about this, "Yes, I thought I'd be alright there but when I'd bought my usual ninety nine with raspberry and chocolate sauce I casually asked him about the Sally and he went all wall faced and instead of joking about my diet like he usually does he told me to; "Go and feed my face somewhere else because I was putting other customers off with my messy eating habits!" Me, messy! I'd only got a little bit of raspberry sauce down my shirt!"

"Yes but maybe it was the chocolate on the nose that did it," Aimee grinned, "Still it does seem a bit strange him changing his tune like that. I mean, if you're such a good customer he must be used to you eating like a pig by now… me and Mum are!"

"Thanks a lot! So what do we do next?"

"Well I think we'll try to go on board the Sally on Friday afternoon. We'll use the bottle and go there a few seconds behind time so that we're ghosts and we'll follow whoever looks most likely to lead us to Walmsley and his dealings. We'll need to get some evidence against him if we're going to get him back for Dad. I wonder if your camera will work and bring back pictures when we're in the past," Aimee mused.

"Talking of Dad, are you going to tell me about him then?" Jamie asked.

"Oh yes, sorry. I've got some great news for you. I went to Dad and he's alive." Aimee gushed, suddenly excited again as her morning came back to her, "He's in a hospital in Italy and he's been in a coma there for nearly two years."

Jamie's face lit up when she said he was alive then clouded when the coma was mentioned. "A coma, two years... so why are you so excited, Aimee? If he's been in a coma for that long he must be really poorly mustn't he?"

"Well yes, I suppose so... but he's alive, Jamie! And if he's alive then we can see him again. They don't know who he is. He was beaten up and all his things were stolen, his documents, money and everything. But we can bring him back here and..."

"And?" Jamie asked to bring it home to his sister that it wasn't that straightforward. "Aimee, he's in hospital for a reason. He is poorly and in a coma and... and he might not come out of it. What will we do with him here? What would we tell Mum... Hey we found Dad but he seems a bit sleepy? Come on, Aimee, we can visit him but if he doesn't recover then he's better off staying where he is."

Aimee's head drooped and she went silent for several minutes before suddenly lifting her head again and announcing, "Come on, Mouse Muck, we're going to visit Dad. It's only three o'clock so we've got about an hour before the glass man returns. Pass me the bottle and hold on tight."

"Before we go, Sis, er... does he look all sort of... er... mashed up?" Jamie asked with a worried, sickly look on his face.

Aimee smiled broadly and answered, "No, he looks like Dad trying to be sleeping beauty! Take me to where my Dad was ten seconds ago please."

116

They arrived in Dad's room just as the door opened and the nurse walked in. Jamie ducked down automatically to hide but Aimee hauled him to his feet again and he reddened as he remembered that she couldn't see him.

The nurse walked over to Dad's drip and checked its flow and then started to talk to him, "How are you this afternoon, Mr Mystery? Are you feeling better? It would be lovely if such a handsome chap as you would talk to me, it would make me so happy."

Jamie looked at Aimee and struggled to keep from giggling but Aimee merely diverted his attention first by squeezing his hand very tightly then by telling him to watch her lips as she spoke. He frowned and was puzzled by this but did as he was told. His mouth fell open when he too noticed that her lips were not saying what he heard, the mouth shape and timing were all wrong.

Aimee watched the expressions on his face as he tried to work out what was happening. After a few minutes she could contain herself no more and asked him quietly, "Well, what do you think then?"

His brow furrowed and then he asked, "You said Dad was in Italy but she seems to be speaking in English... her mouth could be speaking Italian I suppose but how come we hear it in English... unless..."

He shook his hand free of Aimee's grip and immediately he heard the nurse saying, "Da dove vieni? Qual'e il tuo indirizzo?" This time her lips seemed to be saying the words perfectly in time.

He turned to Aimee and asked, "What did she say?"

"She asked him where he was from and what was his address? Have you worked it out yet?" Aimee was bursting to tell him but to her consternation he came out with the answer.

"Well I heard her speak in Italian and you heard her in English, but then you were holding the bottle so I reckon the bottle must change

117

the words around. Its like they have on 'Star Trek,' a universal translator."

"Well done, Scabby," she smiled and then as the nurse turned to leave she continued, "Now what do you think about Dad?"

Jamie looked down at him and thought for a moment then replied, "It's been five years since I saw him and I was only six then so I don't remember a lot of him but I think you're right, he does look a bit like he's trying to be sleeping beauty."

As they both smiled down on him he did something that made both of them jump… he smiled back!

Aimee recovered herself and excitedly asked, "Dad…Dad… can you hear us?"

There was no reply and the glimmer of a smile was soon gone but it had been enough to give hope to both of them but it was Jamie that put into words what both were thinking, "We've got to go now, Dad, but we'll be back soon and when we come we're going to take you home to Mum."

At the mention of Mum another small smile flickered across Dad's lips and Aimee instantly made her mind up. "If we're ten seconds behind real time and you can hear us then you must be affected by the bottle as well and perhaps it will help you to recover. We're going to take you home with us now!"

Jamie gave her a worried look, "What about the people here, they'll kick up a right fuss when they find he's gone. They'll get the police and start looking for him!"

"Yes and they'll be as baffled as they are now about him. They don't know anything about him now so if he disappears it will just add to the 'Mystery Man's' mystery. Right, here we go. Hold my hand, Jamie… Take me ten seconds forward please."

Apart from Dad having moved his head slightly nothing seemed to have happened but Aimee quickly went into action. She went to Dad's side and gently untaped the tubing of the drip and eased out the needle, wiping away the small droplet of blood that formed with the edge of the sheet. Next she took each of the monitor pads off him and the machine set up its high pitched alarm. She quickly grabbed hold of Dad's hand, motioned to Jamie to get hold of his other and holding the bottle in front of her commanded, "Take me home to my bedroom please."

The door of the hospital room burst open as Aimee, Jamie and Dad vanished from it and the nurse and two doctors rushed in to resuscitate… no one! They stood at the end of the bed staring at the indentation in the mattress where 'Mr Mystery' had been. How could he have left the room without them seeing him, it had only one door and there was no window. Doctor Di Piedi even looked under the bed but they had only one thing they could say to the police when they came, "The mystery continues!"

The bottle returned them to Aimee's room and even deposited Dad on to Aimee's bed, though he did have his feet on the pillow. Between them they managed to turn him round and put him under the duvet.

"Well, what do we do now?" Jamie asked, "We've got him back but what do we do with him if he doesn't wake up?"

Aimee could only stare at her Dad and smile but she knew that Jamie was right; their problems had only just begun. Then the doorbell rang and they remembered about the glass man.

"You go down and see him in to the kitchen while I sit with Dad and try to come up with some answers to our little Sleeping Beauty problem."

Chapter 11

Reunited

The glazier took just twenty minutes to remove the remains of the old glass from the rubber seal and replace it with the new sealed unit, and then he gave Jamie his bill and left. Jamie took one look at the bill, grimaced and dropped it on to the kitchen table, "No point in adding to her problems just yet," he thought and trotted back upstairs.

Aimee was sitting on her bed next to Dad, holding his hand. She looked up as Jamie came in and beckoned him to sit beside her. "I've come to a decision. It would be impossible to keep Dad secret from Mum in such a small house and anyway we can't really look after him properly while he's in this state, so I think we should take him back. He was safe from Walmsley there and well looked after; I think that nurse quite fancied him!" she smiled. "We could visit him everyday and when he's better then we can bring him home. What do you think?"

Jamie looked at the tears welling in Aimee's eyes and knew how hard it had been for her to come to this decision. He felt his own eyes start to fill and could only manage to nod his agreement.

"Ok, it's ten to five so we've got about twenty minutes before Mum gets back. I think we should go now so we can sort ourselves out a bit for her." She managed a grin and wiped the tears from her eyes with a tissue and passed another one to Jamie.

"Whatever you say, Sis, you're the boss."

She gave him a little smile, put her arm around his shoulders and hugged him close. "Pass me the bottle and let's get it over with."

"Don't I get a say in this?" The voice was thin and dry but it might have been a shout for the effect it had.

120

Aimee turned and stared at Dad, her eyes opened wide and her mouth even wider in disbelief. Jamie, who had bent over to get the bottle from under the bed, straightened up so quickly that he overbalanced and ended up falling across the room against the dressing table. His head hitting the open top drawer and slamming it shut, doubling the sound and visual effect of the fall.

"He hasn't changed much has he?" The thin voice observed.

"Dad, you're awake!" Aimee finally managed and again her eyes filled and tears broke out into rivulets down her cheeks.

"By heck, you don't half skrike a lot for a big girl! You've grown a bit since I last saw you... but you're still my Aimee, pretty as ever. You couldn't get me a drink of water could you; my throat's as dry as a camel's bottom."

She sniffed back her tears and a broad grin spread across her face, "You've changed though, Dad, you used to say bum!" and she jumped up off the bed to get the water.

"Hi, Dad, I'm glad you're back with us again. I've... we've missed you," Jamie was lost for words for once and that was all he could manage to come up with.

"Hiya, Sprog; hell you've grown as well!"

"Well it has been five years since you saw me you know!" Jamie still felt some anger at having been abandoned by his hero.

Aimee arrived back with the water as Dad responded to his son's unexpected reply.
"Five years... that can't be right can it?" He looked up at Aimee for an answer, he was truly baffled and this told in his eyes.

She handed the glass to him and he drank eagerly, she nodded her head to confirm the five years. Explaining all that had happened to him, and to Mum, Jamie and herself was going to take some time and the threats of Walmsley and Larus had also to be faced up to. Her head was a whirl of worries and she needed time to work her way through them. She also needed Jamie's help so she was annoyed with him for his tetchiness towards Dad and the expression on her face told him so.

"Sorry, Dad, it's just that I… I'm pleased you're back, honest I am!" He tried to make amends but events were getting on top of him.

Aimee knew her brother well and knew how to deal with him. "Why don't you go downstairs and start getting tea ready for Mum coming home… and while you're at it have a think about how we're going to explain Dad's return to her. I think we're going to need one of your super brilliant white lies here Dogbreath!"

Jamie's face brightened a little as he turned to leave; now he had some creative thinking to do he was a lot happier.

"Five years, Aimee?" Dad asked, "Is that right then? Can you help me out a bit only I can just about account for two or three."

"I'll try, Dad. You left us to get some money together to pay off Walmsley and…"

"Walmsley… you know about him then? I wanted to sort things out without you knowing that's why I went. It was for you, you know love, you and Jamie and Sal."

"I know, Dad, but something happened when you were in Italy and you ended up in hospital in a coma. You were in it for two years and they didn't know who you were because whoever attacked you took all your identification documents." Aimee was trying to explain as briefly as she could to get him settled for Mum coming in.

"Italy…So how did I get back here then?"

"That's a good question… and you'll have to wait for the answer… er… Jamie might be the best one to explain everything to you. I'll just go and see if he's alright down there." She turned to go then stopped and turned back to him. "Do you think you're strong enough to walk?"

"I might be ok as long as there are no steep hills, why?"

"I think it might be better if you went to your own bedroom so that I can have somewhere to sleep tonight," Aimee smiled and then helped him to his feet and slowly along to Mum's bedroom where he toppled over exhausted onto the bed.

"Now I believe you, I must have been off my legs for two years for them to feel like this... they're just jelly! And my head's starting to cloud again... I'm..." His eyes closed and his breathing deepened as he fell soundly to sleep.

"Well that solves one problem for the moment. Now to deal with Mum," she told herself. On her way down to the kitchen a thought struck her; Dad had woken up when she and Jamie and the bottle had been with him... when he went to the other room - away from the bottle - he was suddenly tired again. Was it another of the Star Fall's powers helping him?

As she got to the bottom of the stairs she heard Mum's car pull up outside and rushed to the kitchen to see how Jamie had faired. The table was laid out beautifully... for four! Aimee sighed and quickly removed Dad's setting. "We've got to be careful how we tell Mum about Dad. He's gone back to sleep for now so we've got a bit of breathing space."

"It's alright, Sis, I've got everything sorted. I know how to explain everything to her. Now shove this salad on the plates while I finish off cutting the Spam."

The front door opened before Aimee had time to ask what he had planned so she had no choice but to put her trust in him. Beads of sweat began to form on her forehead and she had to sit down as Mum came in.

123

Mum looked at the feast and, and remembering her lunchtime visit began, "Mmm, this looks nice; Spam salad. Jamie's turn was it? No more broken windows I hope? No more visits from the Police, Ambulance, Fire Brigade, Coastguard... International Rescue?"

Jamie walked over to her, took her arm and led her to her place at the table, pulling the chair out for her like he had seen waiters do in posh restaurants on the telly. "Would, Madame care to be seated?" he asked with a flourish of his hand.

Mum looked a little bemused but joined in the act and as she sat down asked, "Would it be possible for me to peruse the wine menu?"

"Certainly, Madame, I will bring it to you shortly." At which point he hurriedly hunted out a pen and a piece of writing paper and wrote out the range. He returned to the table and ceremoniously handed the "wine menu" to Mum.

She scanned the list and pronounced it to be, "A fine selection of excellent quality, if a little limited in its range; tea, coffee or dandelion and burdock... I'll have the tea please."

Aimee was beginning to relax a little and got the cups ready while Jamie put the kettle on to boil and put the tea bags in the teapot. Perhaps he had come up with a half decent explanation after all; he was certainly putting on a great show at the moment and Mum seemed to be getting into a good mood.

They joined Mum at the table and began to tuck in to the salad which Mum said was "Delicious, the chef must be congratulated on his culinary skills." She even expressed delight at the dessert; prunes with long life thick cream. When all was eaten she sat back in her chair and finished off her cup of tea before asking, "Well, what have you two been up to this afternoon then, besides looking after the glazier that is?"

Aimee gulped her tea down and looked towards her brother. What was his brilliant plan going to be? She waited, hoping he would come up trumps and save the day.

"Err…" he began, "Happy Birthday, Mum!"

Now that came as a real shock to Aimee, she certainly didn't expect him to come up with that.

Mum smiled, remembering back to their disastrous visit to the Red House Hotel. "But it's not my birthday."

"Well we've got a surprise for you anyway. Come on, it's upstairs!" Jamie stood up and began pulling Mum up out of her chair towards the door.

Aimee sat in a state of disbelief for a few seconds then got up and followed on behind. "What is he going to do next?" she muttered as she tramped up the stairs.

At the bedroom door Jamie took hold of Mum's hands and said in a soft voice, "Mum, what would be the best present that we could get for you to make up for all the daft things we've done lately?"

She thought for a few seconds before answering, "A four week holiday in Spain on my own without you two. Well… it would be nice if Mike was with me of course."

Jamie looked at Aimee and raised his eyebrows as if to say, "Come on then, let's show her." But she just stood there staring back at him so he carried on with his plan on his own.

"Well, Mum we couldn't afford the holiday, not after the glass man anyway, so we got you the next best thing." And he pushed open the bedroom door.

Mum had thought quickly about what it might be and half expected there to be a sun bed standing in the room so it was a double shock to see her husband sleeping peacefully on the bed in a white hospital gown. Her mouth fell open and she staggered forward a few steps before regaining her balance and her senses. After a period of complete silence, broken only by the gentle snoring of Dad, Jamie came out with the rather unnecessary, "Surprise!"

What Mum came out with was a surprise as well. "Where the hell did he come from?"

It was now that Jamie really showed his creative imagination in all its glory as he astounded both his Mum and his sister with an explanation of mind blowing simplicity. "He was abducted by aliens!"

Aimee could take no more! She gave him a sharp bruising kick on the back of his ankle, grabbed his arm with deliberately pinching fingers and hauled him out of the room towards her own room. As she left she called back, "We'll just leave you two to get to know each other... and I'll fill you in on the details when you've had a bit of time to recover."

Back in her bedroom she pinioned Jamie against the wall, her hands gripping both of his arms tightly. "What sort of brilliant idea was that you cowpat?" she hissed into his face.

"It was... err... all I could think of. Do you think she believed me?"

"Believed you! I don't think even you would be crackers enough to believe you!"

"Oh."

"Oh... is that all you can say? Oh!"

"Err..."

Aimee had had enough, "No more! I'll do the explaining from now on. We'll just say that he turned up on the doorstep not long after the glazier left. He was in a daze and talking nonsense so we put him to bed. We'll not try to explain anything else. I'll have to get to Dad to back us up but hopefully we'll get away with it. Ok?"

"Ok... but I think the alien thing worked alright you know." Jamie persisted before realising his error and ducking just in time to avoid Aimee's hand.

After half an hour of straining her ears to try and hear what was happening in Mum and Dad's bedroom Aimee gave in and went downstairs to be annoyed with Jamie again. At least that was her intention. She found him in the kitchen covered in flour, a mixing bowl in one hand trying to spoon chocolate coloured cake mix into little paper bun trays with the other. The trays moving around the work surface away from his spoon proved too much for her and she stood in the doorway and giggled as she watched him get more on the surface, the floor and himself than he got in the cases.

"What are you doing, Dogbreath?"

"Making buns for Mum and Dad... only they keep running away from me!" he replied in his happy nevertheless voice.

"Why don't you put the bowl down and hold the cases while you fill them?"

"Good idea, Sis, I never thought of that... still there's not much mixture left now so I might as well finish off like this," he grinned.

Aimee shrugged her shoulders, went into the lounge and turned the television on. The news was just ending and the weather man came on; apparently tomorrow was going to be warm and bright with just a chance of some thundery showers.

"Another nice day tomorrow then, Love."

"Mum! I didn't hear you come down, you made me jump."

"Yes, seeing your Dad up there on the bed like that made me jump a bit as well." She closed the door behind her and sat down on the settee beside Aimee. "I've told Jamie that I don't want to see him until the buns are ready with a cup of tea and the kitchen and him are spotless. That should give us time for you to let me know the truth about your Dad, the alien."

"Well actually, Mum, Jamie wasn't too far from the truth really; he just sort of put his interpretation on it," Aimee fibbed, starting the process of keeping Mum from the real truth. Dad did just turn up on the doorstep like that. He came in a taxi; I had to pay the driver forty two pounds from my piggy! Apparently he told the driver that he'd been to a fancy dress party and had banged his head and forgotten where his car was. Anyway, he looked so poorly that we took him straight upstairs. I tried talking to him but all I could get was, "Where's Sal?" and "I'm home at last." I think we should let him sleep a little bit longer then we should try to get him to eat and drink something."

Aimee could tell that Mum was not totally convinced, but at least she accepted that her explanation was more likely than Jamie's. It would have to do because the real truth was even weirder than aliens!

Mum sat quietly for a while then suddenly sat up straight and took control of the situation. "Mike's back, not fully with us, but back and we have to hope that Walmsley hasn't got wind of it. Forty two pounds for a taxi means that he must have come a fair way so the driver's not likely to know Walmsley. We have to keep acting as if Mike's not here which means that I have to go to work and you have to look after your Dad, Jamie as well. You'll have to make sure Jamie keeps to our plans while I'm not here. I know he means well but he's such a … a…"

"Prat?"

Mum started to laugh and relax a bit, "Thank you, love."

"Mum, do you still love Dad?" Aimee asked, the question seemed to come out of nowhere but she was glad she had asked it. She'd seen Mum flirting with other men, the policeman at the hospital and the taxi driver on the way home and she had worried that she had started to give up on Dad.

Mum seemed to read her mind, "Sometimes I needed to be reassured that I was still… still attractive. I'd started to think that Mike might not come home and I'd be on my own for the rest of my life. But when I saw him up there, pale and thin but still my Mike, I knew he was still the only one for me." She wiped the tears from her eyes and smiled at Aimee, "Yes, Aimee, I still love the scrawny old devil!"

The door burst open and in came Jamie, cleaned, changed and carrying a tray of teapot, cups and buns, lots of buns. "Supper's ready!" he announced.

"I'll take some up for me and Dad and see if I can get some down him. You sit and keep Mum company," Aimee said and she winked at Mum as she gathered the tea and buns and then at Jamie as she passed.

Once upstairs she went to her room and took the bottle from under the bed and then went in to Dad. He was still asleep as she entered but within a minute or so of her sitting down beside him on the bed his sunken eyes began to flicker into life and slowly opened. He licked at his dry lips but his tongue was just as dry. Seeing this Aimee ran to the bathroom with the glass from the bedside table and refilled it with fresh, cool water. She lifted his head gently from the pillow with her right hand and carefully placed the glass to his lips and let water trickle between them. After a few sips she put the glass down and wiped away the excess water with a tissue and began again. Dad closed his lips and dropped his head down away from the glass when he had had enough.

"Thank you, precious," he whispered and then his mouth shaped itself into a broad smile as he began to shake with quiet laughter whilst tears formed in his already bloodshot eyes.

Aimee began to laugh too, caught by his infectious smile, "What is it, Dad? Why are you laughing?"

He managed to calm himself enough to explain, "I just remembered holding you in my arms giving you drinks when you were a baby and now it's your turn to look after Daddy!" and he set off laughing again.

"Well if you're feeling up to it Jamie has made you some chocolate buns and a cup of tea. Do you want me to sit you up and feed you some?"

He nodded and helped Aimee by pushing down on the mattress as she hooked her hands under his arms and lifted. She was shocked at how light he was - he had been a big sturdy fisherman when he'd left them. He certainly needed Jamie's buns and a lot more to get him back into shape.

She broke pieces off the bun for him to take in and chew and put the cup of tea to his lips for him to wash each piece down. He managed to get through one and a half buns in this way before shaking his head to say he'd had enough. "We'll try you with some soup later," Aimee told him as she put the remains on to the bedside table.

"Dad smiled, "Thank you, nurse," then his face became serious as he asked, "So come on Aimee, how did I get back here? I was in a coma in hospital in Italy and you managed to get me back here without anyone noticing, not even your Mum. How did you manage that then?"

Aimee held her bottom lip between her teeth and looked down at the floor, then up at the curtains and finally at Dad. "This is going to sound absolutely daft to you, Dad, but I swear it's the truth and Jamie will confirm everything I tell you… But it has got to be kept secret, even from Mum. You have to promise that you will keep the secret or I can't tell you anything!"

Dad looked at her face and especially her eyes that were staring steadfastly into his and he knew she was worried and even afraid, but certainly very, very serious. "I'll not tell anyone, I promise, not even Sal."

And over the next twenty minutes she told him about Thomas, the Star Fall and the bottle's powers. She didn't tell about Larus still being alive or about the gull and its attack on her. That could wait; she didn't want him worrying about her in his fragile state.

"So you can see why it all has to be kept secret, the bottle is too precious to lose. In fact I'm sure its helping you to get stronger now." She picked the bottle up from the floor and showed it to him. It glowed and its colours varied from blue-green to orange-red as Dad reached out and touched it. "Hey, you're having some effect on it as well... but then you are my Dad!"

"And I'm very proud of being so. I'm not certain I can take in everything that you've told me but I do believe you, I really do. Now, didn't you promise me some soup? I think that bottle is making me better you know!"

"I'll go down and open a tin. Chicken or tomato?"

"Chicken please, and some bread and butter if that's alright?"

Aimee smiled and held the bottle up in front of her eyes, "I think I'd better put this back in my room for now, if I leave it here any longer you'll be wanting to go out jogging! I'll send Mum up with the soup she'll be really pleased to see you're getting better and it'll give me the time to go over things with Jamie. Just remember, Dad, you don't remember how you got here but you can remember getting out of the taxi. That should keep Mum off our trail for a while."

"Got it, Boss... and Aimee... thank you for bringing me home."

Chapter 12

Visitor

"Now look, you two," Mum began as Aimee and Jamie sat down to breakfast next morning, "I daren't take any more time off work or they won't let me back in the place. I'm sure if I told Mr Sudworth about Mike being home and the state he's in he would give me some time off, but we print the Red House Hotel menus for Walmsley and we don't want him finding out do we?"

They shook their heads.

"So it's up to you two to make sure your Dad is well looked after while I'm gone. Can you do that for me... for us?"

Jamie, keen to show that he could be trusted, put down his spoon and began to speak, "Of cour..."

"Mouth!" both Aimee and Mum reminded him.

He chewed and swallowed the mouthful of 'Kocoa Krunch' and tried again, "Of course we can; you can depend on us, Mum, honestly."

"Honestly? When was the last time you said, "Honestly"? Don't bother trying to remember I'll tell you, it was last week when you, "Honestly" didn't leave the bubblegum in your trouser pocket when you put them to the wash and ruined them and all the rest of the clothes including my favourite blouse! So don't give me, "Honestly," Jamie Hawthorn, just be good. And you, Aimee, I expect you to be super good to make up for the bits of not good that he does." At this point, feeling that she had got the message across, she smiled and went upstairs to say goodbye to Dad.

"It was an accident! I forgot I'd put it in my pocket for later, it was only just losing its flavour." Jamie continued to protest.

Aimee sighed, exasperated by his lack of understanding of Mums, "Then why did you say you, "Honestly" didn't put it there? If you'd admitted it then Mum might have been a bit more understanding."

"Yeh, like a bird understands what it's like to be a worm!" he sulked.

"Well at least you admit you're a worm," Aimee grinned, "Come on, finish your breakfast, we'll wash up and then go up to Dad and see how he's feeling."

Dad was sat up in bed reading yesterday's paper when they popped their heads around the door and called out, "Good morning, Dad!"

"Good morning Aimee, good morning, Batman."

"Batman, why Batman?" Jamie asked with a puzzled look on his face.

Dad smiled at him and then looked towards Aimee, "It's a pity your sister here can't catch eh!"

Aimee smiled back at him, she'd guessed that Mum had been filling him in on his children's progress over the five years of his absence and that Jamie's "accidents" must have figured pretty highly in her report.

The smiles only got Jamie more confused and he began to get rattled. "Come on you two, why the knowing smiles and why Batman?"

"You've got a short memory Dogbreath, he's talking about yesterday... the window remember." Aimee reminded him.

"Yes but that was Lar... Oww!"

She withdrew her foot from his shin and finished off for him, "Of course it was Lara, you always have to be Brian Lara because he scored 555 in a match and I have to be the bowler because it's your bat," she glared at him daring him to say any more about it at his peril.

"Well at least it's nice to see that the two of you get along so well together. I suppose you've had to help each other out quite a lot with me being away and your mum having to go to work to pay the bills. Sal says she's really proud of you two," he looked at Jamie with smiling eyes, "most of the time. Now what are you going to be getting up to today then?"

"We're going to be looking after you, Dad, making sure you're fed and watered and so on," Aimee answered.

"Now that makes me feel like a gerbil, have you got a wheel for me to run round in as well? I suppose Sal made you both promise to stay in and look after me didn't she? Well I'm feeling a lot better this morning, not up to playing in the cup final, but better. I don't want you two hanging around the house all day, you need to get out and get some fresh air. I'm sure I'll be alright tucked up here in bed for a while so if you want to go out, go… just don't go climbing any lamp posts ok."

Jamie went red and nodded before turning and running to his bedroom to get changed out of his pyjamas.

Aimee waited until he had gone and quietly asked, "Dad, can you tell me what George Walmsley wanted you to do?"

The expression on Dad's face prepared her for what he was about to say. "George Walmsley is an evil creep of a man and I don't want you going anywhere near him for any reason and certainly not to get back at him for what he did to me!"

"But what did he do to you, Dad?"

"That is between me and him and when I'm fit and ready I, are you listening, I will deal with him in my own way, in my own time. Got it?"

"Yes, Dad," Aimee replied looking down at the threadbare bedroom carpet.

"Look me in the eyes, Aimee and promise me that you will not go near Walmsley, ever!"

She raised her head and looked into his eyes, "I promise, Dad."

"Good girl, now if you could pop to the shop and fetch me today's paper and some liquorice allsorts to see me through to lunch I'll be well looked after and you and your brother can have the morning off."

"Right, Dad," she smiled and left him to catch up with more of yesterday's news. As she closed the door behind her she caught sight of Jamie's bright green carpet slipper slipping back into his bedroom and changed direction to follow it.

She pushed open his door to find him sat on his bed pretending to read his bird book. "You heard all that didn't you?" she accused him.

"All what?" he asked, all innocence and smiles.

Aimee merely gave him a short hard stare then ordered, "Make sure Dad's been to the toilet, make him a cup of tea and be ready to go out by the time I get back from the shop. We've got three hours before Mum comes home for lunch and we've got a lot of detective work to do!"

"What about Larus, should you go to the shop on your own?"

"I'll run there and hurry back… and I'll take the umbrella with me just in case. See you Dogbreath."

The shopping trip went without any problems and Aimee was soon back sat on her bed waiting for Jamie to get his camera and notebook for their morning's investigations. Dad was settled down with his newspaper and allsorts and listening to Ken Bruce on the radio. When Jamie finally arrived she told him her plans. "I'm going to use the bottle to go back and follow Walmsley at the last time the Sally came back in."

Jamie stared, amazed at her for lying to Dad. After a few seconds he managed, "But you promised Dad you wouldn't go near Walmsley!"

"Ah, so you were spying on us then."

"I... er... I just happened to be passing and ...er... sort of overheard a bit."

"Yes, well I'm not going to be that near to him am I? I'm going to be a few days behind him aren't I? And even then I'll be a ghost!" she explained and raised her right eyebrow to prompt him to say how clever she was.

Jamie of course was not quite so forthcoming in his praise, "You're getting as sneaky as I am; I think you must be learning a lot from me, Sis."

Aimee closed her eyes and shook her head in exasperation, "What was he like?" she thought. "And you're going to seeing if you can get any more info about the Sally from your friend, Billy. Don't forget to ask about the packages this time eh."

She waited until Jamie had gone then picked up the bottle and was about to ask it to transport her back when a dark shadow fell across the window. She turned and went cold as she saw the gull sat on the window sill staring in at her. She regained her nerve and, still gripping the bottle tightly, walked out of the room and across the landing to see Dad. Hiding the bottle behind her back she sat down next to him and, as calmly as she could, asked if she could have a liquorice allsort.

"Of course you can, sweetheart, help yourself. Aren't you going out then?"

"I will in a bit, I'm just waiting for…"

She didn't have the chance to say any more as the shadow loomed at the curtained window and rapped harshly on the glass with its beak. She pushed herself tight up against Dad and he could feel her body shaking. The gull rapped again, this time harder making the whole window rattle with the force. Dad moved to the right and put his foot out of bed ready to go to the window but Aimee grabbed hold of his arm and pulled him back to her side, looking up at him and shaking her head pleadingly at him.

As suddenly as it had arrived the shadow took wing and left again. The room brightened as the sun was once more allowed to reach the thin blue and white striped curtains. Dad looked down on Aimee and hugged her tight for a few minutes, waiting for the right moment when her fear had subsided enough for him to speak.

It was Aimee though, who spoke first. She knew she had to tell him about the attack on her and about the dangers that the gull posed and why. The words came out in fits and starts as she struggled to cope with reliving her encounters with Larus and his other form, the gull. Fear and misery seemed to be the only emotions that Larus brought with him until with a breaking smile she recalled how Jamie had seen him off, first with the umbrella then by climbing the lamp post and latterly so effectively with his cricket bat.

"So our Jamie is quite a hero then. Try telling that to your Mum!" Dad chuckled.

"He is though, Dad, he's pretty clever as well… when he puts his mind to it. Most of the time he's annoying but I'm quite proud of him really. But please don't tell him I said so, he'd be a right pain if he knew."

137

Dad was silent for a few moments and then he swung himself round to face Aimee. His eyes were moist with tears and his lips trembled a little as he spoke, "I'm so sorry I wasn't around to help you through all this, Aimee. I had problems I had to sort out for myself but I'm back now and if there is anything I can do to help you must tell me."

"Thanks, Dad, but I think getting your strength back should be your first priority so that you can…"

The bedroom door crashed open and Larus stood in the doorway with his hands held ready to grab Aimee should she try to run. "I'm back, Aimee Hawthorn, it was nice of your clever little brother to leave a little window open just for me."

Dad suddenly leapt to his feet and pointed a finger shakily at him, "You, I know you… you were the one that attacked me in Italy. I remember your voice and your… your clothes, your shoes… I remember them kicking me when I was on the ground. You left me for dead!"

Larus let out his hideous cackling laugh then sneered, "Ah, Mr Michael Hawthorn, the father of the brat! I left you for dead because I thought you were dead! I have followed the blood line from Thomas May to you, waiting for the power of the Star Fall to return. When you ran away to that foreign land I had so much difficulty finding you that I thought you must have the power with you. Alas, you disappointed me so I left you there for the local thieves to plunder and returned to watch your little one grow up, perhaps one day to find the Star Fall. And she did and now I will have it back." He held out his claw of a hand towards Aimee, ready to snatch away the bottle.

Aimee stood up and moved towards him holding the bottle tight and close to her side in her left hand. With her right she reached out for Dad's left hand just as he swung his right fist at Larus. His fist slid straight through Larus' head shocking Dad and leaving him feeling sick.

"Nice try but didn't your darling daughter tell you I am only solid when I want to be, and I want to be now!" He swung his arm and knocked Dad backwards to the floor pulling Aimee with him.

Aimee looked quickly at Dad then returned her attentions to Larus who was now leaning forward to take hold of the bottle. She pulled it closer to her and quickly called out, "Take me to my room!"

Dad blinked several times then just stared around him as Aimee pulled him up off her bedroom floor, "Get ready, Dad, we're going again when he gets here… oh and try to remember Jamie's…"

She had no time to finish as Larus burst into the room, "You can't keep this up forever you know, I will always be around waiting for you and I will be a lot less angry with you if you give me the bottle now."

Aimee merely smiled in reply and asked the bottle to; "Take me to Jamie's room."

Again Dad blinked and stared but his attention was quickly gained by Aimee who pointed at the bookshelf behind the door and pushed him towards it just as Larus arrived in the doorway. Aimee took a step back away from him but at the same time lifted her left arm to allow Larus to see the bottle.

His eyes never left the bottle as he advanced towards her, both of his hands in front of him ready to take it.

Aimee took another step back and gulped as her heel touched the wall by the window. Larus smiled in triumph as he saw the fear on her face and moved in to take his prize.

As his hands closed Aimee quickly kicked the slipper off her right foot, dropped the bottle and put her foot on it. As Larus immediately bent over to pick the bottle up she took hold of his arm and said, "Happy birthday!" He had no chance to avoid the pile driver of a shot from Dad who used to play for his school team and still knew how to score a six.

Aimee rushed to try and open the window as Larus once again shrank into a shadow, rose up and made towards it. Unfortunately she didn't move quickly enough and the shadow moved through it and it bulged and shattered.

"He must be quite thick really, that's twice we've pulled that trick on him. I don't know how we're going to explain the window to Mum again though," Aimee said with a cheerfulness brought on by sheer relief. Her cheer was short lived as Dad first grinned at her then collapsed in a heap on the floor.

Aimee turned him over onto his side, bent his right leg with his knee forward to stop him from rolling onto his face and pulled his arms forward for extra stability. "Thank goodness for first aid at the Guides," she muttered as she made sure he hadn't swallowed his tongue. "Right, back to bed with you," and taking hold of the bottle and Dad she asked it to; "Take me onto Dad's bed please."

Once she'd got him settled in under the duvet, she stood back and gazed down on him. He'd been her hero, he'd realised what she'd wanted him to do - what she'd told him Jamie had done - and even though he was exhausted, he had done it. She smiled down at him and was rewarded when he gave a little shake of his head and opened his eyes and managed, "Don't worry about the window, I'll pay for it."

"And how are you going to do that, all you came back to us with was your hospital gown and a smile?" Aimee replied but her words were lost on him as his eyes closed again and he began to snore quietly to himself.

She quickly went downstairs and looked up the number of the glazier and rang him to see when he could come round. Hopefully she might be able to get the window fixed without Mum knowing.

The 'Glassman' laughed in surprise, "What again? Why don't you pair play in the park or on the beach? I bet your Mum really loves you. Ok, I'll pop round and measure up this afternoon. I don't think I can fix it until tomorrow morning but I'll see what I can sort out seeing as you're becoming my best customers. See you at about three o'clock."

The front door opened as she came off the phone and in walked Jamie. "Hi, Sis, have I got some info for you! I've had a smashing time being a secret agent."

Aimee flopped back into the chair and started to giggle uncontrollably.

"What's got into you?" Jamie asked before being infected by the giggles.

"Well I've had a smashing time as well," she managed to splutter and after a few minutes she calmed herself down enough to tell him the story of her morning.

Jamie listened and was excited by all the twists and turns but then when she got to the broken window he just sighed deeply and said, "Brilliant, and I suppose I'll get the blame for it again; I'll be grounded for so long I'll have to have someone to collect my pension for me!"

"Never mind, Granddad, I'll make some tea and we'll go up and sit with Dad till Mum gets back. You can tell me what you found out as soon as she's gone back to work."

Dad was still sleeping peacefully so they sat on the end of the bed to drink their tea. Aimee was about to take another sip when she suddenly remembered what Larus had said. She put her cup down and looked at Jamie in her own special, "You'd better get the right answer or you're for it," way.

Jamie gulped, he knew his sisters looks and this one was one that he hated, it usually meant he was in trouble.

"Larus paid you a compliment when he was here, Jamie; he called you "clever,"" she began.

"Oh yes, er…why do you think he said that?"

"Well I think he was rather pleased with you for helping him to get into the house."

"What! I didn't help him… I wouldn't help him, he's a monster, a villain, a… a creep. How did I help him?" Jamie protested.

"He said you left a window open for him."

"I didn't, honest I didn't. I… oh sugar! The toilet window; I must have left it open after I took Dad there this morning. But it wasn't all my fault, it was Dad's as well; I had to open the window because Dad's er… toilet was… well it was… a bit niffy!" He held his nose and pulled a face to illustrate just how 'niffy.' "I must have forgotten to shut it again when I went out."

"That's right, blame your poor old Dad just because his body isn't back to normal yet," Dad complained with yawn and a grin.

"Well I don't think all this liquorice is going to you help much in that department, Dad," Aimee said as she grabbed the bag and threw a handful to Jamie.

By the time Mum arrived they were quite happily playing scrabble, though there had been arguments over some of Jamie's words. Only he seemed to have heard of 'grumple' and he was sure it had something to do with making paper models of people's heads. Apparently you would grumple the ears into shape. He was so convincing that they let him have its score but they did warn him that they would check it with Mum. To everyone's surprise she backed Jamie up, though she did give him a not so secret wink as she gave her verdict.

"Come on, Jamie dearest, let's go and get the sandwiches and tea while these two have a cuddle," Aimee cooed as she pulled him off the bed and out of the door.

After Mum had gone back to work they tidied away the dishes and, as Dad settled down for another sleep, went into Jamie's room to sweep up the broken glass. "Come on then, what did the defective detective find out this morning?" Aimee asked as she tipped the dustpan into a carrier bag.

Jamie's eyes lit up with excitement as he sat down on his bed and began his account. "I went to the ice cream man and he told me to push off when I started to ask for information as well as chocolate sauce. So I looked for Billy Mackie again and I found him sitting outside the Fisherman's Mission drinking a mug of coffee but it seemed to smell of something stronger, a bit Christmas puddingy. Billy told me that Walmsley sometimes comes to the quayside when the Sally comes in. He has a white van with the Red House logo on the side for collecting fresh fish for the restaurant."

"Well there's nothing suspicious about that, it makes sense for them to get their fish from their own boat," Aimee objected.

"Yes, but it wasn't only fish that he collected. They dropped a tray right in front of Billy once and he says there was something in wrapped in a plastic bag under the fish. He says they covered it over as quick as they could and he pretended not to be looking. And anyway, he says they take a whole vanload of fish at a time - far too much for the restaurant to use."

"So it looks like they're bringing something in that they don't want anyone to know about," Aimee agreed.

"And Billy reckons that's not all, he says that there's always someone that comes in on the boat, helps to load the fish and then goes back with the van. Billy says they're not part of the normal crew; they don't go out with the boat, they only come in!"

143

Aimee looked at her brother's face, he was almost shaking with nervous energy at the discoveries he'd made. She knew she had to bring him back down, to make him see the need for caution and not go rushing in because of the dangers of dealing with someone like Walmsley. They needed to make sure of every fact because they were going to need the police to help them put him away.

"Jamie, we need good evidence so that we can build up a file for when we go to the police."

"The police! But I thought that we were going to get Walmsley!"

"No, Jamie, we have to make sure he is put in prison so that Dad is safe. We have to get as much good evidence as we can, photographs would be great but it would be too obvious if you were down there taking snapshots."

"What about you. You could go back a few seconds and follow them. They wouldn't see you and you could take all the photos we need. You could even see when they hand the stuff over to Walmsley and get a snap of that… I wonder how you could get him to say cheese," Jamie suggested enthusiastically and he pretended to be Walmsley smiling at the camera.

Aimee looked more doubtful, "We don't even know if I can take pictures of the past and bring them back."

Jamie wasn't going to let go so easily, "Well let's try it now, you get the bottle and I'll make sure the batteries are ok in my camera," he ordered.

Aimee shrugged her shoulders and went to her bedroom for the bottle. As she returned the doorbell rang and she remembered about the glazier. "That will probably be the Glassman but will you let him in… just in case."

Jamie looked puzzled, "Just in case?" Then the penny dropped, "Oh… just in case it's Larus!"

Aimee nodded and sighed and Jamie skipped off down the stairs. The glazier didn't stay much longer than five minutes but he made it seem much longer first by his jokey remarks about children being left alone getting up to no good, then by his constant harking on about them being good for business. This wasn't helped when, as he descended the stairs, he told them that it would be Friday morning before he could get back to them and that it would be nearer two hundred pounds as the window was bigger than the one in the kitchen.

"Two hundred pounds! Where are we going to get that from?" Aimee cried as she closed the front door.

"Look on the bright side, Sis; at least you have until Friday to find it. Come on, let's try the camera."

They returned to Jamie's bedroom and Aimee put the camera strap around her neck and held the bottle up saying, "Take me back one minute please."

She giggled as she saw herself walk into the bedroom followed by Jamie and pointed the camera and took her own picture. She checked the picture on the camera view screen gave another little giggle and asked the bottle to return her.

Jamie was surprised to see her back so soon but also pleased, he couldn't wait to see if his idea would work. They looked down at the screen and hugged each other as there looking back at them was the frowning face of someone who had just been told she had to find two hundred pounds by Friday.

Chapter 13

Body Blow

Aimee sat on the edge of Jamie's bed with her head in her hands trying to work out how to raise the two hundred pounds. Jamie's idea of popping into a bank vault to get the money (and perhaps a few thousand extra just in case Larus came round while they were in the greenhouse) was dismissed as being dishonest. His idea of going back to the Red House after closing time in the restaurant, watching while Walmsley put all the takings in the safe, remembering the combination and then returning later to get the money had lots going for it, but Aimee thought it might stir things up too much. They didn't want anything to spoil their big plan of getting enough evidence to put him in jail for as long as possible. Other ideas came and went with the minutes and hours of the afternoon until eventually Aimee refocused her thoughts back on George Walmsley.

She turned to her brother and outlined her plans for his approval: "We know more or less what Walmsley is up to and we know that the Sal' should be back in again on Friday evening, so if we can gather some evidence before then we can get the police to be there and catch them red handed. We need to get pictures of the stuff being loaded onto the Sal' and off again. We need to get as many names as we can and their pictures as well. But most of all we must make sure we get evidence that Walmsley is the one who organises it all so that it's him that gets the blame and not some poor crewman who is being forced to do things for him like he tried to force Dad."

"And don't forget that legally Dad is still the owner of the boat so we have to be careful that he isn't dragged into it!" Jamie added.

"Good thinking, Dogbreath."

"Aimee, why do you keep calling me 'Dogbreath,' I do clean my teeth every day you know."

Aimee looked at up at him and to her surprise it seemed as if he really meant it, he had a pained expression and the tone of his voice was so serious that she immediately apologised, "I'm sorry, Jamie, I didn't realise it upset you. I promise I won't call you it again ok?"

"Thanks, Sis. Now when are we going to get the pictures?" he bounced back, "I can't wait to see his face when the police put the cuffs on him and throw him into the back of the car. I hope he tries to resist arrest and they have to rough him up a bit!"

"Hey, slow down. We need to take things steady so that we don't miss anything out; Dad's life might depend on us you know, Cowpat."

"I think I preferred 'Dogbreath.' So come on then, when do we start and what do we do first?" Jamie scowled.

"Tomorrow morning. When Mum's gone to work and we've settled Dad down, you're going back to the harbour to find out when the Sal's last trip was; sailing to landing. When we know that I can go back and take the pictures while you stay here with Dad. That still gives us two days to put all the evidence together and fill any gaps there might be ready to hand it over to the police by Friday evening. Does that sound about right to you?"

"Fine, but why can't I come with you?"

"Because you're the best one to guard Dad from 'visitors;' we need you to be here for him. Come on, let's make him some tea." Aimee knew that flattery was the best way to get around her brother and, as usual, it worked. Jamie's shoulders rose and he went down the stairs practicing his Kung-fu kicks and punches.

Aimee woke early the next morning, not because she wasn't tired or because she was excited by their plans for the day ahead, but because of the weather. It was summertime on the beautiful north-east coast

147

and the hot sunny weather of the last week had succumbed to the torrential rain and sky-shattering explosions of a spectacular thunderstorm. The windows rattled as the rain turned to hail and the garden outside turned winter white, lit by great flashes of lightning across the black clouded sky. She watched the show for a while then went next door to see if Jamie found it as awesome as she did. He was still asleep and she doubted that he would wake even if she took him and his bed outside into the garden, which she did consider doing just for the hell of it. The plastic film that the Glassman had stretched across the broken window would have kept beat for a marching band and Aimee quickly left her brother to his dreams so that she could close the door to keep the sound from her Mum's ears.

As she made her way to the stairs she could hear Dad talking quietly to Mum and she could also hear Mum squealing at every lightning flash and thunder clap. Down in the kitchen she filled the kettle, "Half past six, time for a cup of tea," she decided and turned the radio on to see if the weather had made the local news.

"The body was found floating in the harbour late yesterday evening by the skipper and crew of the Northern Lass. A police spokesman said that it was too early to tell if there had been foul play and that an autopsy would be carried out as soon as possible. The harbour will be treated as a crime scene whilst investigations are carried out and the police have appealed for anyone who was in the area yesterday evening to contact them as soon as possible. The weather conditions are making travel quite difficult this morning and there are reports of localised flooding coming in from all over the region. Stay tuned for a travel and weather update after this bulletin. The Prime Minister is to visit France for talks later today to try and…" Aimee turned the radio off and took the tray of tea upstairs to Mum and Dad's room.

"Morning, you two, they've found a body in the harbour," she called out as she pushed the door open with her foot, "tea's ready!"

"Thanks, love, whose body, which harbour?" Mum asked as she and Dad sat up in bed.

"Our harbour I think, I missed the start of the report and they didn't say who it was and they don't know if it's foul play yet."

"Those chickens must have some right rough games!" Dad said shaking his head and looking very serious.

Mum turned to him and equally seriously asked, "What do you mean, Mike, what chickens?"

Aimee had to turn away to hide her laughter. "The ones in the news; the fowls that keep killing people while they're playing," Dad said still keeping a straight face.

"No, Mike, you've got it wrong, they mean foul as in not very nice... Oh you..." She smiled and pushed him on his shoulder as she realised the joke he was playing. "I think you might be getting better, Mike Hawthorn!"

"And I thought I was perfect already," he replied with a grin.

Aimee left them and went to tell Jamie about the body. The storm had passed over but still rumbled away in the distance while Jamie still rumbled away in his bed. She left his tea on the bedside table and returned to her own room to drink hers. "Perhaps Jamie might find out who it was when he goes down to the harbour to find out about the Sal's last trip," she thought and settled back onto her bed to wait for Mum to get up for work.

Dad felt much stronger and even managed to get himself down for breakfast, though he was very wobbly on his legs; he was obviously still suffering from the muscle wastage that two years in bed had caused. It was a major lift for the whole family to have him back at the kitchen table though and Mum left for work without any orders or warning; she obviously thought that Dad could cope.

As soon as she had gone, Dad slumped back in his chair and sighed, "I'm whacked! I wish I could get my legs back into shape."

Aimee put on her nurses voice and tutted, "Well, Mister Hawthorn, I think that after all that you've been through you are making a super recovery. Perhaps you ought to be starting to push yourself a little bit more though. A little light housework would do you good; you could start with the washing up... Run, Jamie!" and they made a dash for the kitchen door and away up the stairs.

"Nice one, Sis. I'll go and get myself dressed and be off down to the harbour." Jamie grinned as he went into his bedroom.

"Bring the 'Weekly Reporter' back with you; I want to see if there is anything in it about the body in the harbour. And watch out for Walmsley and don't do anything daft."

"Right oh, Granny!"

Aimee took hold of his arm and in a quiet, serious voice warned him, "I mean it, Jamie. We're getting close to Walmsley's dirty business and we don't want him to suspect anything. It could mean big trouble for us if he finds out what we're up to so don't take any risks."

He stared at her worried face for a few moments and nodded his head in agreement then added, "I understand, Sis, I'll be careful don't worry." At the bottom of the stairs he called through to Dad, "I'm just off down to the shops, Dad, can I get you anything?"

"Liquorice allsorts," came the reply above the rattling of dishes, "Oh and some hand cream, all this washing up is making my fingers go wrinkly!"

"Stop your moaning and get on with it," Aimee shouted down the stairs, "Or I'll stop your pay for idling!"

"I'll tell your Mum how cruel you are to me!" Dad shouted back and Jamie left the house knowing that they were both in good hands.

When he returned two hours later he ignored the greetings of, "Ah, the hunter-gatherer returns," from Dad and "I hope you're going to iron that paper before you bring it to me," from Aimee and instead threw the paper and allsorts on the hallway floor, ran straight upstairs, threw himself on his bed and sobbed.

Aimee and Dad were in the lounge playing a serious game of draughts when he arrived back but the tension of competition was forgotten in their concern for him. Aimee glanced briefly at Dad before pushing the draughts board away and rising from the settee to run up to her brother.

His door was closed but she could hear his gulping sobs through it. She gave a gentle knock and pushed the door open. Jamie had his head buried into his duvet and his whole body shook with the force of his crying.

Aimee knelt down at the side of the bed and leant over to put her arms around him and squeeze him gently. She held on to him until the sobs subsided and he began to calm down enough to listen to her.

"What is it, Jamie, what's happened?" she asked softly.

"The body... the body in the harbour... it's Billy," he managed to say in a hoarse whisper. Then he lifted his head and stared into her eyes, "Billy's dead... murdered... with a knife... in his back. He's dead, Aimee, Billy's dead!"

Aimee slowly shook her head trying to take in his words and work out what it might mean for them. "If Walmsley had anything to do with it, and she was sure he had, then it showed that he would stop at nothing to protect his "business." But why kill Billy? Could it be because he had been talking to Jamie? Surely not... but..." her thoughts were broken by Dad calling up from the kitchen.

"I've made a pot of tea if anyone is interested!"

Aimee stood up at the side of Jamie and stared down into his bloodshot eyes, "We'll get whoever did it, Jamie, I promise you we

151

will. You stay there and try to sort yourself out a bit and I'll explain things to Dad. I'll bring you a cup of tea up in a minute or two, ok?"

Jamie wiped his eyes and nose on the back of his shirt sleeve and nodded in reply before slumping back onto his bed.

When she got back downstairs Aimee found Dad sat at the kitchen table chewing liquorice allsorts and reading the front page of the Weekly News. The headline read; "Local Man Found Stabbed" and she could tell by the worried expression on his face that he had also linked the murder to Walmsley.

"What does it say about the man in the story, Dad?" she asked, trying to give the impression that she knew little about it.

Dad answered without taking his eyes from the story, "It says he was stabbed and thrown into the harbour just after he left the Seaman's Mission about nine o'clock last night. They don't give his name but I reckon that if he was coming from the mission I must know him - they're all ex-fishermen in there. That's about all it says, the police probably won't want to let too much out while they're getting their act together."

"I know who it is, Dad. It's why Jamie is so upset; he is sort of a friend of Jamie's. After he went to the shop he went down to the harbour because it was on the radio this morning and he found out who it was."

Dad sat quietly for a few moments, staring down at the paper and shaking his head slowly before he finally looked up and asked, "Poor Jamie. Who was it?"

"Billy Mackie, he was an old fishe…"

"Billy Mackie! Not old Billy… why would anyone want to kill Billy? He was a smashing old bloke. I used to work with him when I first went on the boats, he fair looked after me did Billy. Why would they want to kill him?" He stood up and walked towards the door still shaking his head in disbelief.

Aimee was startled by his sudden movement, "Where are you going Dad?"

"Up to see Jamie, I want to talk to him about Billy. I want him to know I feel the same as he does about him. It's about time I started being a Dad for him. I'll sit and talk with him for a bit. If you want to go out we'll be alright, just take care, love," he answered with a thin sad smile.

"I will, Dad, I will," she promised and watched as he climbed the stairs using both banister rails to help his weakened legs. As she drank her tea she read the story for herself and realised that it must have been written late last night before much was known about the victim; there was certainly nothing to indicate who might have killed him or why. She flipped over the pages, glancing at the other headlines but not really taking them in. Her mind was on Billy; for his sake and for Dad's and Jamie's she had to go back and find out who had done it.

She decided to get Jamie's camera and use the bottle straight away so she set off up to her room to fetch them. She paused half way up the stairs as she realised that it meant actually watching the murder take place and taking pictures of it, but continued again as she remembered Jamie's tears.

Once in her room she checked that the camera batteries were fully charged and that the memory card had enough space for plenty of pictures. This done she put her trainers and little coat on, put the camera in her pocket and retrieved the bottle from under her mattress.

"Take me to the harbour by the Fisherman's Mission at nine o'clock last night please," she requested and in a blur of light and shadow found herself there.

There was a slight drizzle dampening and cooling the air and the light was just beginning to fade as she looked around the quayside for any sign of the killer. After a few seconds she made out the shadowy shape of a man standing in the alleyway between two of the fish wholesaler's buildings. The door of the Mission opened and out stepped a balding, cheery faced man who's, "Good night all," was replied to with a many voiced chorus of, "'Night Billy, see you tomorrow."

Aimee immediately got the camera ready and followed Billy's movements in the view screen as he walked away from the mission. What happened next happened so quickly that Aimee almost missed it.

As Billy passed the alleyway the "shadow" lurched out and plunged a knife into his back. Billy was pushed towards the edge of the dock and the "shadow" told him, "Mr. Walmsley doesn't like people who talk too much."

Aimee clicked away, taking as many shots as she could and trying to capture the face of the assailant who didn't seem to react to the flashes at all. With a final huge push he sent Billy over into the murky harbour water, holding on to the knife to withdraw it from his back.

Her clearest shot came as Billy's body hit the water with a loud splash and the man suddenly turned and ran straight towards her making her press the button and step aside at the same time. He disappeared into the alleyway again and within seconds she heard the sound of an engine struggling to start and then a vehicle driving away with a screech of tyres.

Shouts came from over the other side of the harbour and she saw several people running around to where Billy had been pushed. At this point she decided her job was done and with a shaking hand she took the bottle from her pocket and asked to be returned home.

Chapter 14

Unwelcome Guests

As soon as she arrived back home Aimee put the bottle back in its hiding place and sat down on her bed to view the evidence. She had managed to get six pictures of the murder, one showing Billy coming out of the Mission, two which clearly showed the side of the murderer's face as he approached Billy and one which showed the actual moment that the knife was pushed in to Billy's body. Another showed both of them as Billy was pushed over into the water. The last showed the murderer's full face as he ran towards the alleyway.

A wave of nausea washed through her body as she stared at the expressions on their faces. Billy's of wild eyed shock and realisation that he was done for and the malicious glare and grin on the face of the murderer. She dropped the camera onto the bed and dashed to the toilet to be sick.

The sound of throwing up brought both Dad and Jamie out onto the landing where they waited for her to come out. When she did her face was pale and her eyes were tired and red. She swayed unsteadily for a few moments then her legs gave way and she collapsed forwards into the waiting arms of Dad who pulled her along to her bedroom and deposited her onto the bed. He sat down on the bed at her side and gazed at her with a worried frown, gently stroking her head and quietly repeating, "Aimee, oh Aimee."

Jamie picked up the camera and started to check the images on the view screen. His eyes widened and he smiled as he saw Billy walking out of the Mission door towards the camera. The next image though came as a complete shock and wiped the smile from his face replacing it with a look of horror. The face of the man walking after Billy was someone that he knew well; it was the ice cream man!

155

Dad saw the expression on Jamie's face and stood up to look over his shoulder at the view screen. "That's Davy Lough, he's one of Walmsley's cronies. He's a right headcase, I hope you haven't been mixing with him!"

Jamie didn't reply, instead he clicked on to the next picture and then on to the next, the murder. Dad took the camera from his hands and quickly turned him round and sat him on the bed next to Aimee. He stared at the image for a few seconds then clicked on to the next two, shaking his head and muttering to himself. Jamie just sat and stared up at him in silence, his head full of thoughts of betrayal and revenge and Aimee. Aimee had seen it all happen and had still managed to take these pictures! He turned and gazed at her, she had captured the final moments of his friend's life and also the evidence to convict his killer. He was so proud of her and it was this more than anything else that brought back the tears that now flooded out of his eyes.

Aimee's eyes opened and she looked up at her brother and comforted him with, "So what are you blubbing for, Cowpat?"

Jamie again said nothing but he fell on top of her and hugged her tightly. Aimee pulled her arms from under her body and wrapped them round him squeezing him as hard as he squeezed her.

Dad gazed down on them and sighed, he didn't really know what was going on, but he was sure that whatever it was these two would do their best to look after each other.

When he finally spoke it was in a tone that instantly conveyed his misgivings, "Come on you two, I think you've got some confessions to make. I want to know what on earth you've been up to. These are pretty serious pictures you've got here, Aimee, serious enough to put Lough away and for him to come looking for you if he gets to know about them,"

"I used the bottle to go back and take them, I can't bring solid things back from the past but I can bring back pictures of what happened just as I can see them. He won't know about the pictures because he couldn't see me, only Thomas could see me because he's in our family," Aimee explained.

"So you think that no one knows about the pictures except us then?"

Aimee nodded, "I'm sure, Dad."

"I hope you're right, it's bad enough having Walmsley after me, but having his chief nutter after you as well would not be a good idea!"

Jamie couldn't contain himself any longer, "But we're going to get both of them aren't we, Sis'?"

Aimee looked sharply round at him and shook her head telling him silently to shut up.

"You two are not going anywhere near Walmsley! I will sort things out with Walmsley, he is my problem...Got it!"

"Yes, Dad, but..." Aimee tried to explain.

"No buts... end of story. I will see to Walmsley ok?" Dad concluded with his finger wagging at both of them. "I'll look after the camera until I've decided what to do. You two get your faces washed ready for Mum coming home, I don't want her seeing that you've been upset; she might start asking awkward questions and I don't want us to have to lie to her. Well go on then, get going!"

As they reached the bathroom door they heard the front door open and Mum's voice call out, "Is there anyone in or have you all been abducted by Jamie's alien friends?"

"We're all up here, Sal," Dad called back, "I'm just teaching them how to wash their faces properly."

"And when did you learn to do that then? Come on get yourselves down here, I've brought you all some fish and chips as a treat seeing as you haven't broken anything for a day or two!"

Dad smiled to himself and knocked on the bathroom door, "Come on you two; fish and chips for being good little children looking after your old Dad and not wrecking the house. And, Jamie, make sure your bedroom door is closed when you come down won't you."

Dad managed to keep Mum occupied in small talk about the printers for most of the time but as she started to get her things together to go back to work she suddenly came out with, "I do hope that you two haven't been at each others throats again, no amount of washing can get rid of red eyes that quickly you know. Whatever it is that's wrong I want right by the time I get back tonight!"

"Oh, they're ok, Sal, it was me that made them cry… I was telling them how we first met and how you told me you didn't want to see me again after our first date. They were so sad that they started crying."

There was a smile in her eyes as Mum responded to Dad's fib, "Well that's nice of them but I bet they're not quite so upset when you tell them the whole story, Mike Hawthorn!" And with that she gave him a kiss on the cheek and set off back to work.

Aimee was smiling broadly and Jamie was giggling as he turned around to face them. "Well come on then, Dad, let's have the full story," Aimee demanded as he sat back down at the table.

Dad grimaced and took a large gulp of tea to give himself time to think. "Well… when we met at that party I thought that Sal was the most gorgeous girl I'd ever seen - even if she did break most of my toes when we were dancing. All my mates thought the same and they were dead jealous when she gave me her phone number and said she'd go out with me. Anyway, when the DJ said it was the last dance and put on a real smooch of a song I held her right close and… well I… gave her a kiss."

Jamie pulled a face and put his fingers in his mouth, "Urrrgh!"

"Ignore him, go on, Dad," Aimee urged.

Dad's face went a deep red as he remembered the event in vivid detail, "Well she seemed ok about it at first but then she suddenly pushed me away and said, "Bluurgh! Your mouth tastes like a chemical works... and your breath isn't any better!" just as the music went quiet. Everybody heard and my mates fair creased themselves laughing at me. I was so embarrassed I just had to get out of there and I ran away from her..."

Jamie was now completely taken with the story and sat with his head in his hands gazing at his Dad waiting for the next bit. Aimee nudged Dad's arm to get him started again.

"We sailed early the next morning and that trip was the worst I ever went on. All those that had been at the party couldn't wait to tell those that hadn't and by the time I got onboard they were all walking up to me and saying things like, "Swallowed a chemistry set have you, Mike," and "I should gargle with 'Estee Lauder' if I was you, Mike!" And I had to take it all because if I'd reacted to them they would have done it even more and there's no place to run to on a trawler. The trouble was I hadn't a clue what to do. I already brushed my teeth twice a day and I even used mouthwash and floss. My teeth were in brilliant condition! It wasn't until we got back and I was still so torn up with anger and embarrassment that I decided I would have to ring her to find out what she meant. I was dead nervous but I was also dead determined to have it out with her. I practised just what I was going to say but when she answered the phone I only had enough time to say, "Hello, Sally, it's Mike from the party..." when she started going on at me because I had left her there on the dance floor and how embarrassed she'd been by me leaving her and how she didn't think she would want to see me again if that was how I was going to treat her. When she finally took a breath I managed to get a word in and reminded her about what she'd said about my mouth."

"And what did she say to that, Dad?" Jamie asked eager to get to the rest of the bust up.

"Well she just said, "I'm surprised a little thing like that got to you, it's easy to cure you know!" and I still hadn't a clue what she was on about so I asked how. She gave a little laugh and said, "Grow up and stop smoking. Just because your mates do it, it doesn't mean you have to." And I was gobsmacked. I mean everyone on the boat smoked at that time; it was just something that you did because... because everyone did. Now I had this mad woman telling me not to because my mouth stank! But then she was really gorgeous and... well... no one had ever spoken to me like that before and it sort of ... made me respect her. She'd been honest with me. It's the best way to earn respect, to be honest with people."

"So you stopped smoking and married Mum," Aimee concluded with a smile.

"Not straight away, she made me wait two years until we'd saved up enough for a deposit on this house. Mind you, getting in the saving habit also meant that I was able to buy the boat nine years later; when you were seven, Aimee.

"The Dancing Sally," Jamie chipped in.

"Yes, the Dancing Sally," Dad smiled and relaxed back in his chair, his eyes slowly closing as the heat of the summer and the effort of telling his emotionally charged story overcame him.

"Come on," Aimee whispered as she stood up and ushered Jamie out of the kitchen into the lounge, "let's have another look at the paper and see if it adds anything to what we've found out."

"But, Dad said we..."

"Dad isn't going to be strong enough to take on Walmsley for some time yet, so we have got to keep on finding out as much as we can for him. Besides it's quite safe, if I use the bottle no one can see me can they?"

160

"I don't think Dad will see it that way," Jamie warned, "But I suppose if we're careful he won't know until we've got everything sorted, eh?"

They began reading through the paper for every mention of the murder and of George Walmsley. Aimee got a pencil and paper and made a note of times and places along with any names that were mentioned. It soon became obvious that they already knew a lot more than the paper did and Jamie started to flip the pages towards the sports sections.

"Hey, look at this, Sis!" he suddenly called out excitedly, pointing to a small advert in the "lost and found" section.

"What is it, has someone found a murderer?"

"No, but someone has lost a dog and they're offering a reward of two hundred and fifty pounds to anyone who finds it!"

Aimee immediately saw what he was getting at, "That's what we need for the Glassman! What does it look like, where and when was it lost and has it got a name?"

"It's a large, black, standard poodle cross, lost on the beach at Covingham on Tuesday evening and it's called Cuddles. Dad can't get mad at us if we go out and find a dog, can he?"

"Especially not if we get the window money for doing it," Aimee agreed and they went back to Dad to tell him they were going out.

After several shakes and nudges they woke him enough to get him to go upstairs and once he was safely snoozing on his bed they went to get the bottle. Aimee was about to request it to take them to Covingham beach when with a shout of, "Wait!" Jamie rushed back to the kitchen and returned a few moments later with an old skipping rope and a pack of sausages.

"Are you still hungry?" Aimee asked and took him by the hand and made her request to the bottle; "Take me to Covingham Beach at five o'clock last Tuesday please."

The sun was now more often than not hidden by a shroud of thin cloud moving in from the north-west, giving a cool end to what had been a perfect seaside day. The beach was starting to empty as the afternoon holidaymakers made their way back up the hill to the car park and away to their various holiday hotels, cottages, caravans and tents. There were a few hardy families waiting for the tide to force them to leave, which it would in the next half hour or so as it was already advancing well up the beach. At the southern end of the beach, by the path that led over the cliff tops a man and a woman danced and shouted, trying desperately to get their dog to come out of the sea.

Aimee nudged Jamie, "I think we've found our pooch, Sherlock; the Hound of the Baskervilles is having its annual bath!"

"How do you know they're called Baskerville, the paper only gave a telephone number?" Jamie replied with a puzzled look.

Aimee just stared at him and shook her head in disbelief, "For a bright lad he could be really dim at times," she thought.

As they watched, the couple whistled, shouted and tried to coax the dog out with treats, but he was obviously having too good a time to be tempted. Finally they tried psychology and turned away from it and started to make their way up the beach towards the car park, occasionally shouting over their shoulders, "Bye then, Cuddles" and, "We're going home now, Cuddles."

By the time they had reached the top of the beach Cuddles had come out of the sea, but instead of following them he had seen another dog, a speedy golden brown mongrel, at the other end of the beach and was rapidly bearing down on it. The mongrel didn't seem to have anyone with it and after taking one look at the sizeable figure of Cuddles thundering towards it decided to use its speed and fled up the cliff path towards Abbsmouth. Cuddles was not easily put off by speed, he had ancestors that were deer hunting dogs and he shared their love of the chase, so he set off in hot pursuit leaving the couple only able to watch and shout from an ever increasing distance. The man started to go after Cuddles but soon realised it was no good and returned to comfort his now distraught wife. They waited around on the beach for another hour or so until the sea reached the car park path and then they sadly made their way to their car.

After first laughing at the antics of Cuddles, Aimee and Jamie now felt really sorry for his owners and were glad that they were going to return him to them. "Right," Aimee announced, "Let's go get him." She took the bottle out of her pocket, took hold of Jamie's hand and asked it to, "Take me to wherever Cuddles the dog is in our time please."

They found themselves standing in the middle of a wood staring at a thick clump of brambles. They turned around and there, standing looking at them with his tongue lolling out of his mouth, was Cuddles. Jamie took a step towards him and immediately Cuddles tongue disappeared to be replaced by a large set of growling teeth.

"Errr... nice dog... good dog," he tried and he held out the back of his hand for Cuddles to sniff.

"GROWFFF!" was Cuddles immediate reply and Jamie's slaver covered hand quickly retreated behind his back.

"Try the sausages, if he's been out here since Tuesday he'll be starving," Aimee whispered nervously.

"You try them, I want to be a rock guitarist when I grow up and I'll need both hands for that," Jamie replied squeakily, "They're in my back pocket; you'll have to get them... my hands have gone on strike for danger money!"

Aimee slowly stepped forward, retrieved the sausages and unwrapped them. She tore one off and holding it at arms length she took another step towards Cuddles, at the same time speaking quietly but firmly to try to calm him down and win his trust.

"Good boy, Cuddles… good boy… here we are, Cuddles."

Cuddles smelled at the sausage suspiciously and then with a quick snap of his jaws the sausage disappeared and he sat down and lifted his paw to ask for more.

Jamie started to relax and brought his hands from behind his back at which Cuddles immediately stood up and growled again. The hands were soon out of sight! It was another six sausages before Cuddles allowed him to move and only then because Aimee had passed him the last sausage to feed to him.

"Right, now we've calmed the beast let's get him back home so we can ring his owners and claim our reward," Aimee said as she made the skipping rope into a noose and slipped it over Cuddles' head and around his neck.

Jamie looked nervously at Cuddles who, even sat down, came up to his chest and then turned to his sister. "Couldn't we just sort of leave him here and tell his owners where he is?"

"But then one of us would have to stay here with him until they got here and it would have to be you in case Larus turns up. You wouldn't want to leave me here on my own for him to get would you?"

He looked again at Cuddles who seemed to be staring hungrily back at him. Jamie knew he was beaten. "Ok, Sis, get us home… and ask to go straight to the kitchen, I think there's a tin of corned beef in the cupboard… and I bet he won't need a tin opener!"

Aimee took the bottle in one hand, the rope in her other and Jamie had to link arms with her as she asked to be returned home to the kitchen.

The sudden change of scene didn't seem to alarm Cuddles in the slightest and as they arrived in the kitchen he simply looked up at Aimee and gave her a paw to ask for more food. She was about to tell Jamie to get the corned beef when the sound of voices coming from upstairs made her freeze and put her finger to her mouth to warn Jamie to be quiet.

The voices - one was definitely Dad's - were arguing. They were not actually shouting, but raised so that they could easily be heard downstairs.

They heard Dad say, "I've told you, I've got the money I just need some time to get it all together, it's stashed in a few different places and I've not exactly been in a position to get it what with your friend here roughing me up and leaving me for dead."

"Yes, well you should have been a bit more cooperative with him shouldn't you, Mike me lad, you shouldn't have tried it on eh?"

Jamie turned quickly to Aimee and mouthed what she already knew, "Walmsley!"

"Try it on! I told him I had all the money and I was coming home with it at the weekend but he wouldn't listen. I think you sent him to do that to me."

"Aye well maybe I did, that's something we'll have to put down to one of life's little mysteries won't we. But now I want my money back and I want it by Friday or you and your family will be out of a home. No money, no house! I'll have my lawyer make up the proper legal documents and I'll be round here with them on Friday... I'll have the money or your signature and if your not here I'll have your signature anyway. I've copied it enough times in the last five years to keep the boat working for me - one more for a house will be easy enough. Ha ha ha!"

"You..."

"Enough of this! I've brought you to him, now it's time for you to keep your part of the bargain, Walmsley. I believe they are downstairs waiting for us now."

"Larus!" Aimee gasped and gripped the bottle tighter, thinking of where she should ask it to take her and Jamie. Then she realised she couldn't go anywhere, not now Walmsley was here and he had Dad. "What do we do, Jamie?"

Jamie stood and stared at her; he had also realised that with Walmsley involved the cricket bat probably wouldn't be enough and even using the bottle would only solve half of the problem. "I don't know… but I'll think of something."

"Could you think quickly please only they're coming down the stairs," Aimee pleaded.

"Let's buy some time… take us up to my room!" Jamie ordered.

Aimee made the request and they were transported to Jamie's room. Cuddles again offered his paw to Aimee but she was too busy listening at the door to notice and Jamie had started ferreting around in his bottom drawer.

"Where are they then, Larus? I thought you said they were down here." Walmsley asked with a voice that was straining with impatience.

Larus gave him a disdainful look and then turned back towards the stairs. "She's up to her tricks again, but it won't do the little fool any good this time. Not now we have her precious father in our grasp. Tie him to that chair and stop your bleating - you make my head weary."

Walmsley took a quick look around the kitchen, pushed Dad down onto one of the chairs and grabbed the table cloth. He ripped the cloth in two and used one half of it to tie Dad's hands behind the back of the chair and the other to secure his feet to the chair legs.

166

"What now then?" He asked and leant back on the kitchen work surface before quickly standing upright again as he realised he had put his arm on to a patch of grease.

"Now we can concentrate on the brats, they won't be much of a problem with the two of us on to them… and if they are…" He looked down at Walmsley's jacket pocket and smiled, "Use that!"

Dad saw the look and then the bulge in the pocket, "If you harm my kids I'll…"

"You'll what?" Walmsley interrupted, "You'll do nothing, and this is why!" In one quick and powerful movement he took the gun from his pocket and swung it into the side of Dad's head with a sickening and bloody smack, knocking him unconscious. "Now where are these brats?"

Larus looked upwards and smiled, "Up there, in the boy's bedroom."

"If I'd known I was going to be running up and down the bleedin' stairs all day I'd have brought some of my lads along!"

"I have told you, Walmsley, what I seek must remain a secret that only you can be trusted with. Now come along and keep vigilant, they are clever little fiends."

Walmsley followed, feeling almost proud to be trusted with the secret until he realised he didn't have a clue what the secret was yet.

As they reached the top of the stairs Larus paused, he remembered the cricket bat and gestured Walmsley to go in front.

Inside the room Jamie was still trying hard to come up with his brilliant plan but his silence gave away his failure. Aimee was faring no better and apart from using the bottle to keep running away, which, she realised, would not help Dad, she also hadn't come up with any ideas.

The quiet that had now fallen on the whole house was broken by the click and scratchy squeak of the door handle being turned. Aimee and Jamie moved backwards away from the door towards the window. Aimee dropped the skipping rope and gripped the bottle white knuckle tight.

Cuddles lifted his nose into the air and began wagging his tail.

The door opened slightly and slowly the black shape of a gun appeared around the edge of it, the hand that held it was quivering slightly and its knuckles were, like Aimee's, white with the tightness of its grip. As more of the arm came into the room the hand swung the gun from side to side.

Cuddles could wait no longer and leapt at the fish and chip flavoured arm, fastening his teeth tightly around it and at the same time crashing his front paws against the door trapping the arm in it both securely and painfully.

Walmsley screamed with both shock and pain and in a reflex action squeezed the trigger on the gun. The bullet smacked into the middle of the wall putting a neat round hole into Homer Simpson's donut.

The noise made Cuddles bite down even harder on the arm and the fingers on the hand slowly opened allowing the gun to drop to the floor.

Jamie rushed forward to pick it up and then just stood looking at it in his hands, not knowing what to do with it. Eventually he looked to his sister for help.

"Hide it under the mattress," she whispered, "I hate guns!"

"Hey, Larus, I thought you said they were only a couple of children!" Walmsley managed to shout, "Well one of them is eating me… Do something!"

"Oh halt thy squealing while I think!" Larus retorted without any hint of sympathy in his voice.

Aimee looked to her brother hoping that he had come up with his brilliant idea, "What are we going to do now, Jamie, we can't stay here all day, Cuddles is bound to let go soon... and what have they done to Dad?"

Jamie simply stared at Homers donut, the gun had shaken him; this was real and they could get hurt... killed! The pictures of Billy kept flashing back into his mind. His breathing became shallow and rapid and Aimee saw the colour draining from his face as he began to sway forwards and backwards. She realised he was going to faint and quickly gave him a push so that he toppled backwards onto his bed. As he hit the bed he gave a little groan, closed his eyes and curled himself up into a little ball.

"Brilliant," She sighed, "Well it's up to you and me now, Cuddles, I only hope you can deal with Larus as well as you're dealing with Walmsley. If only I can think of a pla..." The map of the world on the bedroom wall suddenly caught her attention, or rather one particular part of it did. "Australia! They used to send convicts to Australia," she thought out aloud, "I wonder if they'd mind me sending them one more for their collection. Hold on for just a few more seconds, Cuddles!"

She moved across to the door and took hold of Walmsley's limp and sweaty hand. "Now let go, Cuddles, good dog, drop the baddy."

Cuddles did as she asked and even sat down and held up a paw for her.

"You stay there and guard Jamie, I'll be back soon. Take me to..." She thought of the places she knew in Australia, dismissed Ramsey Street and Ayers Rock and decided on... "Bondai Beach please."

It was dark and there was a cold wind blowing in from the sea when they arrived. The darkness was intensified by a sky full of heavy clouds about to burst. The pictures that Aimee had seen in magazines were always full of sun and surfers but as she quickly realised, afternoon in Britain meant after midnight in Australia and summer was winter.

Walmsley stood and looked around with his mouth wide open in shocked amazement.

"I don't suppose you'll get much of a top up on your suntan but at least you'll get away from it all," Aimee said with much delight, "Anyway, I can't hang around here all night." She let go of Walmsley's hand which had suddenly gone stiff and cold and clammy. The sea was just beginning to lap up against her feet as she asked the bottle to return her to her bedroom and she left him to enjoy his paddle.

Jamie was still doing his hedgehog hibernating impression when she got back and Cuddles was sitting by the door growling.

"Ok, Cuddles, come here. I think it's about time we let you meet Lord Larus and see if he likes you," she whispered and as Cuddles moved away from the door she quickly pulled it open.

Larus was not on the landing as she had expected and after a moments hesitation she moved out of the bedroom, quietly calling Cuddles to follow. She edged her way cautiously downstairs and was about to push open the kitchen door when Larus' voice proclaimed, "Come in, Aimee Hawthorne, come in and see what I am about to do to your precious Daddy!"

The evil in the voice went straight to Aimee's heart causing a chain reaction that raced around her body. Her face became pale with beads of sweat forming on her forehead. Her legs weakened so that she had to steady herself by leaning against the wall. Her hands shook and she had to redouble her grip on the bottle. But her mind kept on working overtime, trying to plan ahead for her meeting with Larus. She knew that her Dad's life might depend on what she did in the next few moments.

"I can feel your fear, Aimee Hawthorne, and it feels good. Are you coming in or do I have to start without you?"

Aimee's eyes closed as the voice stabbed home. "Concentrate Aimee… What would Jamie do… think like Jamie!" she muttered to herself. And then she was ready.

"Cuddles, come here and sit," she ordered as quietly as she could manage and still make him understand. Cuddles did exactly as he was told. "Now stay," she ordered, pointing her index finger at him to emphasise the command. Her heart was beginning to settle a little now giving her legs and hands more strength. With a last wag of her finger at Cuddles she turned and pushed open the door.

Dad was sitting in the chair with his feet and hands tied to it. His head lolled forwards and there was blood streaming from a wound to the left side of his forehead. On top of his head sat a large black and white gull with a small knot of hair trailing from its beak. The gull turned its head to look at Aimee as she stood in the doorway, her legs now beginning to lose their strength again.

With a toss of its head the gull threw the hair onto the floor at Aimee's feet. It then spread its wings and with two flaps rose up from Dad's head and hovered momentarily before blurring to a shadow and re-emerging as Lord Larus.

She again had to steady herself against the wall as Larus began to run his skeletal fingers over Dad's head. He let one finger dip into the wound and then held it up and looked at it. "I have had this blood on my hands before. It is the blood of Thomas May and it is also your blood, Aimee Hawthorne. And I will do to you what I did to May… unless you give to me what is rightfully mine!" He knew he had the upper hand now and with a flourish brought his other hand from Dad's head and held it out ready to accept the bottle.

171

Aimee stared first at the blooded finger then at the thin, evil smile that Larus wore so confidently. The detestation she had for him overcame any fear that was left inside her and, though her heart continued to beat hard and fast, she was quite calm as she stepped forward with the bottle.

"At last you are seeing sense, little Aimee Hawthorne. I have waited too many years for this moment but finally I am about to realise the full power of the Star Fall!"

Without once looking away from his face she clutched the bottle tightly and lowered it down towards the waiting grasp of Larus' bony, yellow-skinned hand.

Larus' lips began to quiver as he felt the bottle touch the palm of his outstretched hand and he quickly closed his long, sharp fingers around it and Aimee's hand which had not yet released it. He raised his eyes to meet Aimee's stare and suddenly realised that she did not intend to give up the power so easily. He opened his mouth to issue another warning but did not have time to as Aimee's other hand clamped down on his and she called out, "Now, Cuddles!"

Cuddles bounded into the room and leapt at Larus, knocking him backwards and pinioning him against the kitchen wall. He had his front paws on Larus' shoulders and his growling mouth right into Larus' face… and Larus was no longer smiling.

Aimee snatched the bottle away and warned, "I wouldn't try turning into a gull; Cuddles likes gulls even if their feathers do tickle his throat on the way down!"

"You will pay for this treachery, Aimee Hawthorne, you and all your family. I will not rest until I have what is mine and until I have had my revenge on you!" As soon as he had finished speaking his form began to fade and Cuddles let out a little whimper of surprise as his paws moved through Larus and rested against the wall. The brown shadow that was Larus moved away towards the garden door leaving Cuddles bewildered but still propping up the wall.

Aimee also moved towards the door, getting there first and opening it wide to allow Larus to get out and calling after him, "Goodbye, Larus and remember, we'll always be ready for you... you haven't beaten us so far and you never will!"

Larus' shadow transformed into a gull and rose up into the afternoon sky. He wheeled around and dived down low over Aimee in a show of bravado, screeching down at her, "I will always be watching and waiting, Aimee Hawthorne... My day will come!" before soaring away towards the cliff tops.

As she stood watching the shrinking form of the gull finally disappear over the rooftops Cuddles barked and she returned to the kitchen.

Cuddles sat by Dad, licking at his hand and Dad started to come round, blinking as daylight and pain filled his head. At the same time Jamie stumbled through the hall doorway and with a groan sat down opposite Dad.

Aimee looked up at the wall clock. "Ten past four! Mum will be home in an hour and just look at the state of you two. How do I explain you two to her? Well at least we haven't got any more broken windows..."

"Woof!"

"...Just a massive great dog!"

"And a bullet hole in my bedroom wall... oooh my head hurts" Jamie moaned.

"So does mine... What have you two been up to? And where has this donkey of a dog come from?" Dad managed to croak, "Any chance of a cup of tea before you start to explain... it looks like it might be a long job?"

"Here, hold this against your head," Aimee said and gave the bottle to Dad before going to fill the kettle at the sink. "And you go and give your head a good splash with cold water and I'll see if I can find the paracetamol for you," she ordered Jamie.

"Yes, nurse."

"Doctor!"

"Huh, some sisters are never satisfied."

When he returned, Aimee and Dad were sitting dunking digestive biscuits in their tea and Aimee was explaining about Cuddles.

"So you see, Dad, Cuddles is a lost dog and when we return him we'll get enough money to pay for the window."

Dad looked at Cuddles who took this as a sign that the biscuit in Dad's hand was for him. With a joyful "Woof!" he stood up, put his giant paws on the table and with a quick swing of his head took the biscuit and swallowed it with one crunch and a lick of his lips. He then sat down again and wagged his tail happily.

Dad looked at his saliva covered fingers then at Cuddles, "You say his name is Cuddles... is his owner a bear? What kind of dog is he?"

"The advert said he was a standard poodle cross," Jamie answered, "I think he might be crossed with a wolf... A woodle!"

"Here we are," Aimee smiled at Jamie and handed over two tablets. "Take one now and you can have another later if your head still hurts. I've told Dad about Cuddles - you tell him what happened with Walmsley while I go and phone about the reward. There's plenty of tea in the pot if you're interested."

"Walmsley! I told you not to go near him!" Dad started to shout.

"We didn't go near him… he came near us. But don't worry he isn't near us now." Aimee interrupted as she stood up to go to the telephone in the lounge. "As you seem to have lost your memory a bit you'd better let Jamie explain what he knows so be quiet and keep that bottle on your head. I'll fill you both in on the rest when I get back."

"Yes, Doctor," Dad smiled.

As she made her way into the lounge she could hear Jamie's excited voice telling Dad how they had come home to find him fighting with Walmsley but; "Walmsley had a cosh and a knife and a gun and a machine gun, but Aimee and Cuddles managed to overcome him and throw him out!"

"And what were you doing while this battle was going on then?" Dad asked, "It's not like you to miss out on something like this."

Jamie blushed and looked down at the floor, "I… er… sort of… got knocked out when Walmsley burst into Aimee's bedroom. He must have caught me with his fist or something when he was trying to get out of the way of my kung-fu chops!"

"Ah, and I suppose it was Walmsley that tied me to the chair with the tablecloth… I wonder how he did that when he was fighting Aimee?" Dad mused.

"Oh… er… I might have got some bits mixed up. Perhaps Larus tied you up."

Dad sat forward in his chair, "Larus! Was he here as well? How did Aimee cope with him? What's Walmsley doing with Larus? If they've teamed up together we're in deep trouble!"

"Don't worry about Larus, I've, or rather we've sent him packing for the moment." Aimee could barely keep from laughing as she walked over to Cuddles and gave him a hug. "I'll tell you about Larus and Walmsley in a minute, first we've some more pressing problems. How do we pay for the window and how do we explain to Mum that we've got a new member of the family?"

Jamie and Dad looked puzzled then Dad asked, "Didn't Cuddles belong to them then?"

"Oh yes, he belonged to them alright. But it seems that when they got home to Cheltenham they decided he might be a bit too large for their flat after all and they've bought a cat instead," Aimee explained, "And they said we can keep him if we like… well they actually told me he was my problem now and then put the phone down."

Cuddles looked up at Aimee and lifted a paw, Dad leaned back in his chair and sighed and Jamie simply smiled, threw Cuddles a biscuit which disappeared with a crunch, and said, "Well he's not having my bedroom!"

"And what about Walmsley and Larus?" Dad asked, although they now didn't seem quite as threatening as they had - explaining Cuddles to Sally was a much more daunting task than dealing with them.

"Well, Cuddles persuaded Larus to leave. He apparently likes dogs even less than cricket bats! And I used the bottle to take Walmsley for a paddle on Bondai Beach." Aimee quickly explained.

"Bondai Beach? Where's that?" Jamie asked.

"Australia," Dad answered with a smile.

"Australia? It'll take him ages to get back from there. Well done, Sis!"

"No it won't. He'll have his credit cards and probably a mobile phone so he can ring home and get them to send his passport to him and then hop on a plane back. He could be back in three or four days… a week at the most," Dad reasoned. "Still it gives us some breathing space. Now we've just got your Mum to deal with! We'd better get things tidied up and ourselves cleaned up."

"You go and sort your room out, I'll see to the kitchen, and, Dad, go and wash your face and try to do something with that cut. If you keep hold of the bottle it might help to heal it a bit… I'm getting to like being a doctor." Aimee grinned.

Chapter 15

Plans

"Right then, it's five o'clock and your Mum will be home in about twenty minutes so has anyone got any suggestions as to how we're going to persuade her that we need to have a dog the size of a donkey staying with us?" Dad asked and then looked at Jamie as he added, "And I want sensible suggestions, we haven't got time for little green men!"

"It worked last time... sort of," Jamie complained half-heartedly and both Dad and Aimee stared at him and shook their heads. "Well she almost fell for it!"

"At least the bottle has done its work on your head, Dad; there's only a bit of redness there now," Aimee said as she took the bottle from him and put it in her pocket, "But what about the money for the window, we've still got to find that before tomorrow morning?"

"First things first, Aimee," Dad responded, "Let's settle the Cuddles problem and then we'll have the rest of the evening to see if we can come up with the window money. Any ideas yet?"

There then followed twenty minutes of silence broken only by the heavy sighs and whooping of Cuddles chasing things in his dreams, his legs running and his eyes flickering as he lay stretched out under the table. It didn't help their concentration much but at least it endeared him to them even more.

The front door opened and Mum called out, "I'm home if anyone is interested... and I'm sure it's not my turn to cook tonight!"

Before they could warn her or stop him, Cuddles was up and out from under the table and skidding across the kitchen floor to greet this intruder who had stopped him from catching a rabbit. They met in the hallway. Mum screamed, dropped her bag and for some reason put her hands in the air as if she was being held up at gunpoint. Cuddles; not expecting to be screamed at in such a manner, stopped right in front of her and for some reason rolled over onto his back and waved his paws in the air waiting for his tummy to be tickled.

Aimee and Dad reached the door first and started giggling at this sight, but it was Jamie who immediately seized the opportunity and as he pushed past them into the hallway he went into full fib mode.

"Ah, Mum, I see that you and Cuddles have met. Isn't he a cutie and so easy to look after. I promised my friend, Harry that I'd look after him while he goes on holiday because the kennels he was supposed to go to have had to close suddenly because of some sort of infection. I told him you wouldn't mind and I thought he'd be company for Dad and might even protect him from Walmsley if he ever came round. Dad loves him don't you, Dad?"

"Oh…er yes, he's a lovely dog."

"And he does tricks! You should see him beg for biscuits," Jamie went on.

"And he makes sausages disappear," Aimee couldn't help chipping in.

Mum had lowered her hands by now and looked at each of them suspiciously before bending and tickling Cuddles' tummy. She knew there was something they hadn't told her but she also knew when she was beaten. "And just how long are we supposed to look after him for?" she asked.

"Er… I think Harry said he was going for about three or four weeks, I think." Jamie tried.

"Three or four weeks! Where has he gone to, Australia? Or haven't you thought about that yet?"

"Er… no, I mean yes… yes I think it is Australia. He's got an aunty there and he's gone to help out on the sheep farm… it's shearing time and she needs some help because… because she's getting old and she can't bend down so much any more and the sheep are too fast for her now and…"

"Enough, Jamie, you can keep the dog but only if you promise not to let 'Harry' bring you any sheep back!" Mum smiled and then turned to Dad and let the smile slip as she warned, "I'll get the truth out of you later!"

Dad gave her a nervous little smile and then looked down at Cuddles as he replied, "Oh, he's a lovely dog though, Sal, it's just a shame he hasn't got a nose."

Jamie was puzzled by this remark but Aimee knew her Mum and Dad well enough to expect what followed.

Mum put on an expression of surprise, "He's got no nose; how does he smell?"

"Awful!" Dad and Aimee called out together and burst out laughing with Mum joining in, leaving Jamie looking at them in bemusement.

"But he has got a nose… and he doesn't smell that bad." He knelt down beside Cuddles and sniffed at him before pulling a face, "Well perhaps he could do with a bit of a wash!"

"Never mind, dear, he can get in the bath with you after we've had that wonderful dinner that you and Aimee are going to cook. I think there are some sausages in the fridge, sausage and mash would be lovely thank you," Mum decided when the laughter had died down. Dad pointed at them and grinned but his amusement didn't last as Mum continued, "Come on, Mike, we'll go into the lounge and you can tell me the truth about Cuddles."

Once they had gone Aimee looked at her brother, who was still trying to work out why they had been laughing at Cuddles, and said,

"Well, Brainbox, what are we going to do now seeing as our dinner's in the dog?

Jamie thought for a few moments and then clicked his fingers and announced, "We shall have, 'Sausage Surprise!'"

"But we haven't got any sausages," Aimee reminded him.

"Yes, that's the surprise… it'll really be egg and chips!"

"Ok Dogbr… Cowp… Jamie, you peel the potatoes while I…"

"Lay the eggs?" Jamie interrupted.

"Read the 'Reporter' again," Aimee continued, "There might be something else in the lost and found column to help us with the money."

"Oh yes," Jamie laughed, "And what are you going to bring back this time, a pussy cat that's really a sabre toothed tiger?"

At the mention of, 'pussy cat,' Cuddles suddenly stood up and ran to the garden door, barked twice, decided he couldn't be bothered and went to sleep under the table again.

For the next half-hour Jamie peeled, chopped, cracked and fried while Aimee studied the paper. She ringed several likely advertisements with her pencil and managed to keep an eye on the chip pan at the same time. They both decided that a good portion of baked beans would help divert attention away from the missing sausages. Finally Aimee put the paper away and got the table set up, not forgetting to put a new tablecloth on it first. Luckily Mum had bought two of the same design in the sales so one going missing might not be noticed. With everything ready, Jamie went through to the lounge to announce that, "Dinner is served!"

Mum didn't even mention the missing sausages which left Jamie a bit disappointed that he couldn't do his, 'sausage surprise' joke. He

181

was cheered up though when she complimented him on his 'perfect' chips. After dinner they all went into the lounge to watch the local evening news programme. The police still had no clues about who killed Billy and were appealing for witnesses.

Aimee and Jamie both looked across at Dad who, after making sure Mum was watching the screen, put his finger to his lips and gently shook his head and then mouthed, "Not yet."

Mum suddenly turned to Dad and asked, "Didn't you used to know Billy Mackie?"

Dad's eyes began to fill with tears as he thought back to the times when Billy had helped him as a young deckhand in the vicious North Sea storms, cheering him and geeing him along, getting him through until the boat was safely back home. And he had befriended Jamie and shown the same kindness toward him and Davy Lough had killed him, for what? "Yes I knew him… he was a good man, a good friend."

"I wonder why anyone would want to do that to him," Mum continued, turning back to the screen for the next item of news.

Jamie stood up and ran from the room. Dad followed him and it was left to Aimee to explain that they both counted Billy as a friend. Mum closed her eyes and sighed, "Sometimes it feels as if every way I turn there's something rotten happening and it's just waiting for me to find it."

"Things will get better, Mum, I promise they will," Aimee consoled and she wanted more than ever to tell her about the bottle and her plans to get Walmsley and see to it that Dad was safe and could get his boat back and they could be a safe, happy family again. But she knew she must keep the secret for now and hugged her Mum instead. "It'll be alright, Mum, I know it will."

Cuddles came in from the kitchen, heaved himself up onto the sofa beside and on top of Aimee, squashing her even closer to Mum.

"I see he's made this his home then, I only hope he hasn't got an expensive appetite to go with that belly of his," Mum commented.

"Oh, I think he'll eat anything really," Aimee answered.

"But he especially likes sausages eh?" Mum grinned and they settled down to watch 'Emmerdale.'

The programme was mostly uneventful with just the usual family arguments that any TV soap thrives on, and when the adverts arrived Mum suggested that Aimee make; "A lovely cup of tea," ready for the second half. Aimee trotted off to the kitchen and made enough tea for everyone. Putting the mugs on a tray with what was left of the biscuits, she returned to the lounge to find Mum with her head on Cuddles' bottom quietly snoozing. Cuddles didn't seem to mind and made little snoring noises himself. She carefully put Mum's mug on the coffee table and made her way upstairs.

She stood and listened outside Jamie's door for a few seconds before giving it a gentle kick and calling out softly, "Tea and biscuits anyone?"

"Yes please," came back the reply from both of them and she pushed open the door to find Dad at one end of the bed and Jamie at the other with a mass of pictures and papers in between.

"What are you two up to?" Aimee asked as she put the tray down on the dressing table.

"Dad's been showing me pictures of the crews he's sailed with and the boats. Look at this one," he dug in the pile and picked out a creased old photo of three fishermen posing at the side of a boat called, 'Queen of the Seas.' He smiled and said, "I bet you can't guess who they are."

Aimee took the photo and studied it carefully. She knew that the man on the left was Dad because she'd seen old pictures of him before, and she guessed that one of the others, probably the older one

183

in the middle, must be Billy. But the one on the right, older than Dad but younger than Billy, had her stumped.

"Well… I think that handsome one on the left is Dad… and that one might be Billy… but… no I give in. Who is the other man?"

Jamie's eyes sparkled as he told her. "You're right about Dad and Billy and the other is…" he paused and looked across at Dad before going on. Dad nodded and he continued, "George Walmsley!"

"You were friends with Walmsley?" Aimee gasped.

"Aye, sort of. He was… is a couple of years older than me but we joined the crew of the 'Queen' at the same time. Walmsley had moved into the town with his Mum a couple of months before that photo was taken and Donald Dewer, the skipper of the boat, took us on together. He didn't last long though; three trips and he got seasick on every one and just didn't come in for the fourth. He went back to stay with his Dad in Dunrose and we didn't see him again until he and his Dad bought the Red House. It was a right dump of a pub at that time and stayed that way until suddenly they were able to spend a fortune on it. Nobody knew where the money came from but there were plenty of rumours. Some right shady characters used to drink in there!"

Jamie couldn't contain himself any longer, he had heard all of this already and he wanted to get on with the real business. "We've worked out a plan to get him, Aimee!"

"A plan?"

"Yes, Dad and me have worked out a brilliant plan to get Wamsley and Davy Lough arrested."

Dad chipped in, "If you think it's alright that is. It does sort of depend on you doing most of the work with your bottle thing. Jamie assures me it's safe and that no one can see you when you go back in time, so I suppose you can go near Walmsley after all."

184

Aimee took a big drink of her tea and looked first at Jamie and then at Dad, "Go on then, what do I do?"

The basic plan was just as she and Jamie had thought up earlier; go back and visit the Dancing Sally and take lots of pictures. But in the new plan she was to take in the whole of the trip so that they found out who and where the contacts were and to get the whole operation. She had to make sure she got all the crew's faces and the ones that loaded and unloaded the goods. Then she had to see what happened to the goods and take pictures of anyone else involved.

Once the evidence was gathered they would send it to the police anonymously and wait for Walmsley to be taken away.

When they had finished Aimee took another mouthful of tea, swallowed and then pronounced judgement on the plan. "It's a nice neat plan but I'm afraid you've missed one or two little details."

Dad and Jamie looked at each other, frowned and then looked back to Aimee for an explanation.

She smiled and began, "Firstly, what about you, Dad? The Sally is still registered in your name and so the police will want you as well as Walmsley. Secondly, when the Sally comes in on Friday Walmsley will still be in Australia. Not a bad alibi eh? Even if he didn't know how he got there."

Jamie's eyes began to fill again but Dad was quick to respond, "On your first objection don't forget I've been away for the past five years and in hospital in Italy for the past two, so if you do go back and take pictures of a few trips over that time I can prove I wasn't involved. The hospital will be sure to be looking for me; I can say I woke up in the night and left of my own accord and hitch-hiked my way back here."

Jamie's eyes dried and then lit up as he joined in the dismissing of Aimee's objections. "And you could fetch Walmsley back in time for the boat coming in. If you went tomorrow afternoon it would be the

185

middle of the night in Australia and you could bring him back in his sleep. He'd wake up in a right tizzy and then the police will come for him and what could he say?"

"Brilliant!" Dad enthused.

Aimee was less certain. Dad's 'Italy' story had a few loose ends but she couldn't think of any other objections except that the plan seemed to involve her being up most of the night going too and fro through time. Still it was a small price to pay if it all worked out alright.

"Ok, let's give it a go. Dad, you keep Mum out of the way. Jamie, you make sure the camera batteries are fully charged and the memory card is clear - you'd better dig out spares of both just in case. Oh and don't forget to take Cuddles for a walk before bed time."

"Can't you take him, Sis; I'm going to be busy getting the pictures of Billy downloaded so the card will be ready for you?"

"Oh don't be such a wimp! I'm going to bed for a couple of hours. Night, night." And before anyone could object she left them to it.

Although she was warm and comfortable Aimee couldn't manage to drop off to sleep. She kept going over the plans they had made and some things didn't seem to work out right. Dad hitching back from Italy in just a few days didn't seem realistic, it would take much longer she was sure. And where did he get the clothes from, he could hardly travel all the way from Italy in a white hospital gown without people thinking he was bonkers and calling the police! She decided to change one or two things to make the plan more believable. Jamie's plan for Walmsley was brilliant though. She went over it three or four times and still had to smile as she imagined him suddenly finding himself waking up in his front garden at Scowcroft in the middle of the afternoon in his pyjamas… hopefully he would be wearing pyjamas! Jamie had come up trumps again - he really did have a good brain when the little green men weren't around. She eventually gave up on sleep and decided to go downstairs to see if Mum was awake yet.

Mum and Dad were snuggled together on the sofa watching a James Bond film. Aimee arrived in the middle of a car chase that seemed to involve 007's car doing some really silly and probably impossible things. But Dad was enjoying it!

"Where's Cuddles?" Aimee asked when the adverts interrupted the action.

"He's taken Jamie for a walk," Mum smiled, "Have you come down specially to make us a cup of tea? That's nice of you dear."

Dad looked up and winked at her, "I think we'll all turn in when the film's finished - that is if Jamie manages to persuade Cuddles to come back!"

At that moment they heard the back door open and the padding of paws on the kitchen floor. The door then closed and a few seconds later a red faced and panting Jamie opened the lounge door. "Cud...dles ... saw a ... cat and ... chased it ... I couldn't ... let go of ... the lead ... and he dr ... agged me right ... down to the ... park."

"I suppose you'll want a cup of tea as well then," Aimee said without the slightest note of concern, "Have you fed Cuddles yet or did he manage to catch the cat?"

"What do we feed him?" Mum asked, "Nobody has been to the shops for any dog food yet as far as I know."

Dad stood up and took a five pound note from the sideboard drawer, "Jamie, nip down to the corner shop and get him a tin of meat and some dog biscuits. That should do him until we can do a proper shop for him tomorrow."

"Why me?"

"Because you're the only one who can outrun a hungry dog! Go on, we'll give you ten seconds start."

Seeing that any further arguments were useless he turned and headed for the front door. When he got back ten minutes later he was swinging a carrier bag of dog food and chewing on a very large chocolate bar and had a packet of crisps and comic shaped bulge up his shirt. There wasn't much change from the five pound note.

Once the tea, film and dog food were finished, Mum announced bedtime and Aimee and Jamie bounded up the stairs to get the equipment ready for a night of evidence gathering. She actually felt she was a bit like James Bond only a lot more sensible. She would keep out of the way of the baddies and not keep getting caught and bashed about by them.

"Right, here's the camera, two sets of spare batteries and spare memory card," Jamie told her, "You'll have enough room for about a hundred and sixty pictures, which should be enough."

Aimee looked at the camera and then at Jamie, "I hope this all works out as we hope it will, it'll be great to have Dad properly back with us and not having to worry about Walmsley all the time. Right I'm off back to my room. As soon as I think Mum and Dad are settled down I'll get started. Bye."

"Sis…" Jamie said, his face showing his concern, "take care."

As she sat on her bed, listening and waiting, the bedroom door opened and Dad's face appeared, "Good luck, love, take care."

Aimee gave a little smile then silently shooed him away and settled down to wait again.

A few minutes passed and the door was pushed open again. Cuddles padded his way across to the bed, jumped up onto it and curled up and within a minute or two was gently murmuring in his sleep.

"Well that should do it, I'll be off then," Aimee whispered to herself, and taking the bottle from her pocket she asked it to; "Take me on board the Dancing Sally ten seconds behind our time please."

The Sally rocked gently under her feet as she found herself standing at the prow end looking back down the length of the deck. The only light she could see was in the wheelhouse, illuminating a tired looking man with a sea-worn, stubbly face. All around her was darkness; even the stars were hidden by an overcast sky. She was just about to ask to be transported to another time when the stubbly man suddenly shouted, "They're here!" and there was a flurry of activity accompanied by shouts of "Get the hold open!" and "Make sure you check the trays, we were one short on the last trip!"

Aimee's heart started to beat faster as she saw another boat coming out of the darkness and realised that this must be the place that they took the goods onboard. She switched the camera on in flash mode and began taking pictures of the crew in action making sure she caught each one's face clearly and moving around the boat to get the best positions.

When the other boat came into range she took pictures of its name, or rather number, PH 118, because that was only marking she could see. She continued to snap away as it came alongside and her crew swung tray after tray of packages covered in black bin liners across to the Sally. Each one disappeared down into the fish hold as soon as it arrived. Peering over the side of the hold she could see more men stacking them neatly so as to get as many in as possible. At the other side of the hold were trays of ice covered fish which the men used to cover the bin liners as they stacked each tray. The whole operation took just thirty minutes and was concluded by one of the Sally's crew throwing a small brown canvas case over to the other boat. This was opened and checked and then the two crews simply nodded to each other and the PH 118 pulled away. Within a few minutes she was swallowed by the night.

Aimee had plenty of evidence for the police ready for this trip coming in tomorrow evening, now she wanted to get pictures of past trips going back to when Walmsley took over the Sally. "Take me back to another meeting with this boat six months ago please," she asked and found herself being thrown about the deck by a winter storm.

Again it was night and again, with great skill, trays were being passed across to be stacked in the hold and camouflaged with herring. But this time it was not the only exchange. When all the trays were safely stowed away five men were brought up on the deck of the PH 118 and with little thought for their safety were told to jump to the Sally. Aimee managed to get pictures of them with their terrified faces as they made their leaps and somehow landed safely on the deck to be hauled away and hidden below. This was followed by one man making the jump in the opposite direction and then the passing over of the brown case which Aimee presumed contained money to pay for the goods.

She made two more forays back to previous trips; the last one being just weeks after Dad had gone away. Not once though did she see Walmsley on board. "Probably too scared to do the dirty work himself," Aimee decided.

Finally she rounded off her night by getting pictures of one of the trips being unloaded and caught Walmsley on the dock side supervising the operation. She even got pictures of him pushing the human cargo into the back of a Red House van. She boarded it and photographed the transfer to another van in a lay-by on the A1 just below Newcastle, getting pictures of the drivers and of both vehicles number plates."

"Well, that should be enough to convict the slimeball," she decided, "Will you take me back home to my own time now please."

It was ten to five when she arrived back in her bedroom but she wasted no time in taking the camera through to Jamie who to her vast surprise was sat on his bed, fully dressed, waiting for her. "Hiya, Sis, did you have a good trip?"

"Brilliant! Here get these downloaded, printed off and ready to send to the men in blue," she grinned and then her expression changed as she remembered that she had one more job to do before she could finish for the night.

She tiptoed back on to the landing and stood listening to the sounds of the house; Jamie was fiddling with the computer, Cuddles was whooping after rabbits again and in their bedroom Mum and Dad were gently snoring. Carefully, she opened their bedroom door and crept to Dad's side, shook him awake and with her hand on his mouth beckoned him to follow her. Once out on the landing she whispered in his ear and he went back into the bedroom and re-emerged with the hospital gown he'd worn in Italy.

"Put it on and come into Jamie's room, we need to take some pictures of you for your alibi," she whispered and went in to explain to Jamie what she was going to do.

"Are you sure we really need this?" Dad asked as he came into the room a few moments later.

"Oh yes you need that alright, doesn't he, Jamie?"

"Yes, Dad, you really do need that," he agreed, "Now, Sis, you just make sure he's stood right while I take the pictures."

Aimee took him by the shoulders and turned him in a few different positions then took hold of his hand, put her other hand onto the bottle in her pocket and said, "Take me to an empty room in the hospital we got Dad from please."

"What the hell are you playing at, Aimee?" Dad shrieked as they found themselves in a small white-walled room with a sink and toilet bowl at one side and a door at the other.

"Keep your voice down, Dad and I'll explain," Aimee whispered. "Look, if the police interviewed you and you told them you'd hitch-hiked back from Italy in just a few days wearing only a hospital robe what do you think they would say? Alright they could check up on your hospital story but the rest would make them pretty suspicious don't you think? But, if you let the staff find you here in the hospital and you tell them you woke up and were frightened and confused so you've been hiding from them, it might be a bit more convincing."

Dad nodded his agreement with her reasoning then asked, "But what about your Mum, what are you going to tell her?"

Aimee thought for a moment and then came up with, "The truth… or as much as she needs to know anyway. I'll tell her you've decided to go back to Italy to recover the money you've been saving up so that you can pay off Walmsley. But we'll worry about all the twiddly bits once Wamsley is behind bars ok?"

"I suppose it'll have to be ok seeing as I don't seem to have much choice in the matter. So what do I do now then?"

"Now you have to convince the staff here that you've been hiding around the hospital. I should imagine that they will have been a bit embarrassed at losing a patient so they won't kick up too much of a fuss. Perhaps if you go out of here and stagger around a bit then collapse in front of someone it might help. Anyway, it's up to you now… Take me home please!" And she returned to Jamie's bedroom leaving Dad to stagger out of the ladies toilet.

"You've got some brilliant snaps here, Sis!" Jamie gushed as she reappeared, "Do you think Dad will be ok back in Italy?"

"Well at least he shouldn't come to any harm in the hospital. They'll probably ask him a few questions, give him a check-up and then hand him over to the British Embassy to be sent home. Now, you get those into an envelope and I'll deliver them to the police station. The sooner we get them there, the more time they'll have to set up an operation to get Walmsley and his cronies."

"Good thinking, Sis… and I'll put a note in saying the Sally gets back in later today," Jamie added.

"Ok, but make sure you type it, we don't want them tracing it back to us... you'd better be careful how you handle the pictures as well, don't put any fingerprints on them." Aimee warned.

"Don't worry, look." He held up his hands; he was wearing washing up gloves.

Aimee smiled at him and turned to leave the room. She stood on the landing for a while listening to her Mum's slow, heavy breathing, occasionally broken by a murmur of unintelligible dream chatter. Somehow, despite the lack of sleep, she felt wide awake and ready for the day ahead. There had been too much to think about and do to feel tired.

She looked out of the landing window towards the sun which was just beginning to appear over the North Sea horizon turning the sky a glowing red. "Red sky in the morning, Walmsley's warning," she whispered and then froze as down in the street she saw a man dressed in jeans and dark blue sweatshirt; the same clothing that Davy Lough had been wearing when she saw him kill Billy. It brought the scene vividly back to her and again she saw the knife and the push into the water.

As she looked again the man looked up at her and their eyes made contact. It was Davy Lough!

She immediately turned and rushed back to her bedroom, sitting down heavily on the bed and putting her head in her hands and muttering to herself, "How could he know it was her? He couldn't possibly know... could he?" She strained to work out what he was doing there. Then it came to her. "Jamie... He knew Jamie and he must have seen him talking to Billy. And if he was in the pay of Walmsley then Walmsley could have told him where Jamie lives. He could be here to make sure Jamie didn't find out anything from Billy. He could be here to kill Jamie!"

Her thoughts were brought to an abrupt halt by a large wet tongue investigating her right ear! As she lifted her head, Cuddles put his large, heavy paw onto her knee, looked her straight in the eye and gave out a low sad moan.

"What is it, Cuddles? What do you want?"

He gave another moan, clawed at her leg with his paw and then turned and padded towards the door. He turned his head and gave another moan before going out onto the landing and down the stairs. Aimee knew that he wanted to go out for his morning walk, and judging by the moans he needed to. She decided to let Jamie know that Lough was outside; he had to know to be able to avoid him she reasoned. But he mustn't let his anger make him do anything stupid, not now that they were so close to nailing both Lough and Walmsley.

She got up from her bed and went first to the top of the stairs and called quietly down to Cuddles hoping not to rouse Mum, "Ok, Cuddles, we'll take you in a minute. Try to hang on, there's a good dog." Then she went in to see Jamie.

"Hiya, Sis, I thought you'd gone to bed."

"Jamie, listen there's something we've got to talk about," Aimee said in a quiet serious voice that immediately told Jamie something was wrong, making him drop the envelope he was stuffing with photos and sit up straight. "Jamie... Davy Lough is outside."

The expression on his face changed from one that was excited at the prospects of the events ahead to one of rage and hate. His shoulders rose and he clenched his fists tightly enough for the knuckles to turn white.

"Jamie, I know what you're feeling but you must stick to our plan. He's a paid killer and he'll think nothing of killing any one of us if he thinks we're up to something that will get him caught. Now he's here for a reason and that can only be that he's after either you or Dad... or both; Walmsley must have phoned him to let him know where we live.

194

If you can calm down enough to have one of your brilliant ideas, now would be a good time for it.

There followed a period of silence and then Cuddles gave another, more urgent moan. Aimee left Jamie deep in thought and went down to open the back door so that Cuddles could go out and get some relief. The garden was surrounded by a thick privet hedge and had a high gate at the side of the house so there was no way he could get out. She closed and locked the door and returned upstairs.

As she entered his room, Jamie looked up and said quietly, "I think we need Mum's help on this one, Sis."

Aimee's eyes widened and she was about to go through all the reasons why Mum had to be kept in the dark about Dad and Walmsley and Billy and not least the bottle when Jamie raised his hand to stop her and began to outline his plan.

"Look, Sis, Dad is safely stowed away in Italy and hopefully on his way home soon. We have a really good plan to get Walmsley and Lough behind bars but unfortunately Lough is probably going to kill us first. You could use the bottle to get him away like you did with Walmsley but that would mean two people telling the same story about the power you have and then there would bound to be some sort of investigation and you might lose the bottle. You could use the bottle to get us away but then you would either have to tell Mum and take her as well or we would have to leave her behind and Lough might get her. So we have to tell Mum all about the pictures and our plan, but if we can we'll leave out the time travel thing. I don't think she'd believe that!"

"So what do we ask her to do about Lough?" Aimee asked, still a bit doubtful about telling Mum but impressed by his reasoning once more. Perhaps he was going to come up with the masterstroke.

"I don't know… perhaps Mum will come up with something," was his disappointing reply.

"You don't know what?" The voice came from behind them and belonged to Mum. "Well come on then, what have I got to come up with? And while I'm trying to solve these little mysteries, here's another one for you; where has your Dad gone?"

A loud, "Woof!" from the garden gave Aimee the excuse to gain a bit of time to think. "Oh, Cuddles... I'd forgotten I'd let him out into the garden. Let's all go down to the kitchen and Jamie can make a cup of tea while I let him in." She suggested as she dodged past Mum and ran down the stairs.

"Mmm... I'll go for the tea but don't you think you're getting away from giving me some answers." And as she was about to leave she saw another couple of little mysteries to ask about, "And what on earth has happened to your window... and why is there a hole in your wall?"

"Tea first, Mum!" Jamie replied as he copied his sister's escape technique. He did pause on the landing though and, hiding his face behind a curtain, looked out at Davy Lough standing by the lamp post gazing up at the house.

By the time Mum arrived in the kitchen Aimee had briefed Jamie on what to tell her; which was nothing. He was to leave the explaining to her and to agree and nod in all the right places on pain of a bruised shin.

She decided to begin with Dad. "Dad has gone back to Italy because he's got a lot of evidence hidden away there that could get Walmsley put away and perhaps get the Sally back. He had to go last night because a friend of his, one that he met in Italy, was flying back there in his private jet," she began.

Mum looked dubiously at her and asked, "But why didn't he tell me all this then?"

"Well… he was going to but then Billy Mackie was murdered by one of Walmsley's men and he decided that he had to do it secretly so that they wouldn't come after us…"

"So why has he told you all this and not me?" Mum interrupted, her eyes beginning to fill with tears at Dad's obvious lack of faith in her.

"Because we were at home with him all the time and we overheard his phone conversation with his friend… and, well… I went out down to the docks the night Billy was murdered and I saw it happen and took some pictures of it!"

Jamie staring eyes went from Mum to Aimee and back again, even he was shocked by this admission… and he knew about it.

"You did what?" Mum exclaimed, her mouth falling open in astonishment.

"Show her the photos, Jamie."

Jamie ran up stairs and returned with the pictures within seconds, dropping them on the table in front of Mum and then going round to whisper, "He's still there," in Aimee's ear.

"We'll have no more secrets here my lad… Who's still there?" Mum ordered in a low firm voice.

"The man in the photographs," Jamie answered, his anger beginning to show in his voice again, "The one that killed Billy… my friend Billy… Davy Lough!"

Mum spread the pictures out on the table and swallowed as the truth and seriousness of their story hit home. "And the window, the hole in the wall?"

Aimee didn't hesitate with her reply, "Walmsley came here looking for Dad. He had a gun and he fired it to warn us what would happen to us if we didn't tell him where Dad was… He was hiding in the

197

cupboard under the stairs. The bullets went through the wall and the window!"

Jamie was amazed at how she had so nearly told the truth and yet missed out so much. Mum wouldn't have believed her if she had told the whole truth, of that he was certain. Time travelling with a bottle, Larus the bird man! Who would believe that?

Mum sat and stared down at the pictures on the table and then closed her eyes and asked, "So what is it that you finally trust me enough to want my help with?"

"We need to get these pictures to the police and they mustn't know they came from us or Walmsley will be sure to have someone come after us even if he ends up in prison. But first we need to get past Lough and he's out there waiting for us," Aimee explained, the anxiety beginning to show on her face.

"So who do you think that man… Lough, is after - you or Mike?" Mum asked, still trying to get a grasp on what needed to be done.

"Me!" Jamie exclaimed, "I used to talk to Billy down at the docks and I used to buy ice-cream from Lough so he must have seen me with Billy and now he thinks I know too much and he wants to bump me off!"

"Bump you off?" Mum repeated, wondering where he had picked the phrase up from.

"Yeh, he's killed Billy and now he's coming for me!"

"Or Dad, remember Walmsley thinks that Dad is here so he might have sent Lough to get Dad," Aimee added.

The room was silent as Mum sipped her tea and thought things out. They watched her head nod and shake as she went through plans and weighed up their potential. Suddenly there was a thump against the garden door followed by scratching so vigorous that the whole door began to shake. Jamie ran and hid behind Mum who sat upright in her chair and stared at the door handle, waiting for it to turn. Aimee stood up cautiously and moved towards the door.

"Aimee, What are you doing?" Mum shrieked.

Aimee continued towards the door and with her hand on the handle turned to reply, "Letting Cuddles back in!" The door burst open and in shot Cuddles, skidding on the tiles, wide-eyed and tongue lolling, plodding around the kitchen and wanting to greet everyone with a sloppy lick. "I'll give him his breakfast before he eats one of us."

"Right, I think I've hit on a plan," Mum declared when everyone was settled at the table again. "Aimee, you go and ring the police and tell them there is a strange man hanging around outside the house. When they come he is sure to make himself scarce then we can go out and deliver the photographs. I'll go and get dressed while you do it, simple see!" and she stood up and walked towards the stairs.

Jamie looked at his sister and rolled his eyes, but Aimee did as she was told and returned two minutes later. "The phones gone dead, I think he's cut the wires!"

When Mum came back down she was dressed for work. "Jamie, go and wash your face you're coming with me. Aimee... Aimee what are you looking at me like that for?"

"He's cut the telephone wires, we can't call the police."

Mum smiled, "Yes, I thought he might... shame we haven't got a mobile phone really... still it was either a mobile or the car we can't afford both on my wages. Never mind, it's just as well we've got plan B. Sit down you two and I'll fill you in. As I said, Jamie is coming to work with me. We'll walk quickly to the car and drive off as smartly as we can. If he wants to follow us he can do, but there are a lot of very big men working at the printers and at the time I arrive they're usually in the yard getting the lorries loaded. As for you Aimee, you are going to take Cuddles here for a very long walk. Keep away from the house for as long as you can. I think that..."

Jamie suddenly sat bolt upright and exclaimed, "But what about La... Oww!"

Aimee looked sharply at him as she pulled her foot back under her chair.

"What about who?" Mum asked with a puzzled expression.

"Nothing Mum, I thought I thought of something but apparently I didn't so it doesn't matter." Jamie answered and looked down at the table to hide the tears forming in his eyes.

"Right... I'll make sure the photographs get delivered, Jamie can do that on the way to work if we're not being followed, and I don't think we will be."

It was Aimee's turn to look puzzled now. "Why not Mum?"

"Because I reckon he's after your Dad and he'll break in here looking for him when we're out and as he isn't here he'll be disappointed won't he. If the police are any good they'll look at the photo's and have Lough caught by the time you get back here, Aimee my dear. I'll ring them from work about the strange man just to put them on the right track. Now, does that all seem to make some sort of sense to you? Good, now let's get going."

Jamie gathered the photographs together and shot off upstairs and returned with a bulging large, brown envelope. He turned to Aimee as Mum went into the lounge for her handbag, "Don't worry about Mum's fingerprints, I've put some copies I made in the envelope. The ones Mum looked at are in one of my secret places so Lough won't see them."

"Good thinking, Bruth."

Mum returned, stood with her back to the door and addressed her children like a general on the eve of a battle, "Now remember you two; keep calm but walk out quickly and don't let on that you know he's there. If he thinks we're acting normally he will carry out his plan and not panic and disappear. Then our plan will be underway."

"You're really good at this, Mum," Jamie grinned, his fear of Lough blown away by his Mum's confident attitude.

Mum smiled back at him, "Stick with me kid and I'll show you how it's done."

She opened the front door and there stood facing her was Davy Lough.

"Going somewhere babe?"

"Babe?" Mum winced and in a sudden movement of her right arm brought her fist straight up to meet Lough's jaw with a resounding, "CRACK!"

Lough's eyes rolled up to look at the sky and he staggered, took two small steps backwards and collapsed in a heap on the driveway.

"Babe? He'll not call me that again in a hurry! Right kids, plan C… same as plan B but the police should have an easier job."

Chapter 16

Nearly

Mum stopped the car a little way before the Police Station and watched as Jamie sauntered towards it with the envelope. As he reached the car park he noticed the CCTV cameras positioned above the doors watching all who came and went. He was just about to turn back when a patrol car turned in, parked and its driver leapt out and ran into the station.

Without hesitating, Jamie moved swiftly to the car, opened the door and dropped the envelope onto the driver's seat. Mum drove up alongside him as he got back to the road and he quickly got in and they moved away.

As they turned down St.Anne's Road, Mum looked in her mirror to check that they weren't being followed. Only then did she relax and with pride in her voice she said, "Well done, Jamie, well done."

Jamie stared straight ahead, he had heard the praise but something else was bothering him. As they neared Sudworth's he suddenly sat upright and called out, "Stop!"

Mum stamped hard on the brake pedal and both she and Jamie lurched forward and were caught by their seatbelts. The red delivery van that was following swerved and the driver sounded his horn and showed that his grasp of sign language was as good as his ability to pull angry red faces.

Mum said nothing but turned to Jamie for an explanation.

Jamie undid his seatbelt and quickly informed her, "Slight change of plan... you carry on, Mum, go to work and make the phone call but I have to get out here." And with that he got out of the car and ran off across the park towards the shops. With a shrug of her shoulders, Mum continued on her way to work

Although it was still only a quarter to nine the holidaymakers were beginning to take their places on the beach ready for the warm day ahead. Aimee coaxed and pulled Cuddles along the sand away from the windbreaks and sunshades to the empty southern end where a large concrete wall separated the beach from the harbour. With her back to the wall she could see all along the beach and make sure she hadn't been followed or could be taken by surprise by Walmsley's men. Satisfied that she was safe she sat down and, with Cuddles curled up beside her, began to go over what had happened and what she hoped would happen.

As the sun rose higher in the cloudless sky the beach filled with more and more whooping, digging, paddling and snoozing holidaymakers. The warmth made the snoozing infectious and soon first Cuddles then Aimee succumbed to the wonderful waves of sleep. The lead dropped from her hand and she slowly, gently keeled over to come to rest with her head on Cuddles' back. His deep rhythmic breathing rocked her boat-like into dreams of sailing the seas with Dad at the wheel, and Mum calling out orders, and Jamie scrubbing the decks.

A yapping Yorkshire terrier somewhere at the other end of the beach made Cuddles' ears stand on end; his nose twitched and he was off! Aimee's head hit the sand and she struggled into wakefulness, still wanting to sail around the tropical island just one more time. As she wiped sand from the side of her face she caught sight of Cuddles ploughing his way through the crowds sending towels and picnic baskets flying and scattering children and adults alike. As the Yorkie ran in a circle, weaving in and out of the sunbathers trying to escape, so Cuddles followed creating mayhem and panic.

Aimee, now fully awake to the unfolding pandemonium, ran along the beach shouting, "Cuddles…Cuddles, here, Cuddles… come here,

Cuddles!" to no effect other than mystifying victims and onlookers alike as to how such a monster could be called 'Cuddles.'

As the tired and terrified terrier gave up and rolled over with his little legs kicking in the air, Cuddles stood over him and to gasps and screams, lowered his head, opened his mouth and started to lick him. The terrier squirmed, flicked himself back onto his feet and, now yapping happily, started chasing Cuddles in and out of the windbreaks.

Eventually Aimee caught up with them and at the fourth attempt, dived and managed to grab hold of Cuddles' lead. Deciding that there were too many to apologise to individually she shouted, "Sorry!" as loud as she could and dragged Cuddles away to the nearest exit from the beach. It happened to be the steps leading past Scowcroft to the top of the cliffs. It was a route she didn't really want to take but the arrival on the beach of two uniformed council officials made any other way out of the question.

As they reached the top step, Cuddles started to pull her again, this time towards the section of cliff where Thomas' cottage had been. About a metre from the edge he stopped, sniffed the ground and started to dig. Soil and stones flew backwards at Aimee as she moved to his side to see what was in the hole he was so rapidly making.

A glint of silver in the bottom of the hole soon became bigger and rounder and Aimee gave a little squeal of delight as she realised what it was.

"Leave!" she ordered and to her amazement Cuddles brought his head up out of the hole and sat down, his nose and front paws covered in red muck and his tongue lolling from the side of his mouth. "Good boy!"

Dropping to her knees and leaning right down into the hole she began to scrape away the earth from around the sphere, the Star Fall. Once she had enough room to get her fingers around and under it she carefully raised it to the surface and rolled it onto the grass. As she did so a shadow passed overhead and looking up, Aimee saw the silhouette of a large gull wheeling above her.

Fear and panic took over and she stood up and started to run along the cliff tops. Cuddles sat where he was and watched. He didn't understanding why she was running until the gull swooped down and landed a dozen or so paces in front of her; then he set up a fierce barrage of barking.

The gull grew shadowy and swelled upwards to become Larus. "Well here we are again, Aimee Hawthorn, and no little boys to help you. I see you have my property with you," Aimee's hand went immediately to her trouser pocket, "I think it's about time you gave it to me."

"Never... See him off, Cuddles!" Aimee shouted.

Cuddles growled, lurched forwards and leapt at Larus who simply stood and smirked as the dog passed straight through him and landed in a bemused and whimpering heap at the other side.

"Now can I have my Star Fall power?"

Aimee took the bottle from her pocket and held it in front of her face, the oily liquid inside glowing with a beautiful array of colours. "Take me to..."

Larus held up his hand and said calmly, "Before you do that, let me show you another little trick. It might make you change your mind."

He turned and walked around to the other side of Cuddles who merely looked up at him and whimpered pathetically. He knelt down on one knee and put his right hand to Cuddles' side and allowed it to enter the dog's body. Aimee shivered at the sight and a well of nausea began to form in her stomach.

Larus liked what he saw and, with a cruel smile, he continued, "I have but to close my hand around the cur's heart and he will breathe his last breath. However, we could always make a bargain… the bottle for the heart. A fair swap I believe."

Aimee stared at Cuddle's sad face. She had no choice. She lowered her hand and was about to toss the bottle to Larus when she caught sight of Jamie along the path behind him. He was standing by the hole holding the sphere under his left arm. The lid of the sphere was unscrewed and lay on the grass at his feet. He waved his free hand and gestured to her to throw the bottle to him.

She swung her arm back and called to Larus, "Alright, you have your bargain." With all the skills she had learnt from bowling in school rounders games, she brought her arm forwards and launched the bottle. It flew just high enough to make Larus stand up and stretch with both hands to try - and fail to reach it. His eyes followed the flight of the bottle teasingly past his fingertips and into Jamie's right hand.

Larus, livid with rage, strode towards Jamie. "I will not have any of your silly games, boy, give me the bottle now!"

As Larus approached Jamie raised his hand, just as Larus had done to stop Aimee, and then he bent over and placed the sphere on the grass beside the lid. With both hands together he held the bottle over the open mouth of the sphere and with a "clunk" dropped it in. Looking up at Larus he said, "We've had enough… it's all yours. Now will you leave us alone?"

"No, Jamie!" Aimee screamed, with tears streaming down her cheeks.

"At last!" Larus gloated and as he moved forwards his shape shrivelled to a shadow and the shadow entered the sphere to collect its reward.

Jamie grasped the lid and quickly screwed it down into place on the sphere. He stood up triumphantly, holding it above his head as if he had just collected the World Cup and shouted, "Gotya!"

"Jamie, what have you done… he's… he's got the bottle in there. Now he's got all of the power and nothing will stop him. He could get out of there any time he wants to and then what will he do?" Aimee protested, hardly able to find the words in her shocked state.

"Oh I don't think he'll be too much of a problem now, Sis." Jamie replied quite calmly, "I think we've got him where we want him." And then he explained, "Do you remember what Thomas said about the sphere protecting and imprisoning its secret? Well now we've got Larus in his own little prison. I think Thomas told us that so that we would know what to do with him."

"You know, I think you're getting too clever for your own good Dogbreath!" Aimee smiled and wiped her eyes and then her nose on the back of her arm.

"I've got a handkerchief if you want one… you can borrow it if you stop calling me names."

"Sorry, I forgot. Yes please…Jamie."

Jamie put his hand in his pocket and started to pull the grubby piece of cloth out and with it came the bottle, dropping onto the grass and shining in the sunlight. "Oh, I forgot about that. Do you want it back now?"

"How… how did you do that? Aimee gasped; her mouth wide open in disbelief as she stooped to pick it up.

"Dad showed me some magic tricks while you were out the other day… that's the first time it's worked though!"

A whimper from Cuddles brought them back to earth. They ran over to him and knelt on the grass beside him. His breathing was shallow, his nose pale and dry and his big, brown eyes looked dull and lifeless.

"Oh, Cuddles... come on, it's alright now... Larus has gone. Come on, please get better," Aimee pleaded, lifting his head and stroking his chin.

"He can't die, Aimee, he mustn't die... Do something, Aimee!" Jamie cried.

"Do what! What can I do? What can I... Oh you stupid girl..." And she placed the bottle on Cuddles' chest and moved it in little circular motions, massaging its power into his heart.

"Come on, Cuddles... come on," Jamie whispered as tears ran from his eyes and dripped from the tip of his nose onto the dog's face.

Cuddles' eyes closed as he took in a great lungful of air and then breathed it slowly out again before becoming completely still. He just lay there... lifeless... the tip of his tongue poking out between his dry, tightening lips.

And then he took another, smaller, intake of air. This time his nose twitched and began to turn moist and black. His back legs began kicking at the grass, then his front legs kicked as well and he jumped to his feet knocking both of them backwards and he was off along the path, down the steps and across the beach, ploughing a curving path through the sunbathers as he homed in on the Yorkshire terrier.

Jamie remained on his back, laughing and crying and shaking with a mixture of fear and joy.

Aimee managed to calm herself enough to stand and watch Cuddles' progress along the beach with a huge quivering smile on her face.

"Right, Jamie, you collect Cuddles and take him home," Aimee eventually ordered as she spotted the council officials once again striding down the sand, "I'm going to get Walmsley back to face the music!"

"But what about the sphere, we can't just leave it here for someone to find... they might open it and let Larus out," Jamie reminded her as he finally got to his feet.

"Mmm... you're right... I think I'll take it home and hide it in one of your secret places. I've got an idea what to do with it but we might need a bit of help from Dad. Pass it here and get after Cuddles quickly before those council men get there first."

"What council men?"

Aimee gave him a wink and quickly asked the bottle to take her to her bedroom. Once there she found an old carrier bag to wrap the sphere in and then went to Jamie's bedroom to throw it up onto the top of his wardrobe to nestle amongst his old teddies, models and football magazines. "There we are, Lord Larus, you can keep Pooh, Spiderman and David Beckham company for a while. Take me to George Walmsley in Australia please."

It was nearing midnight as she arrived in the squalid, smelly room that Walmsley had managed to rent while his passport was on its way from Britain. She looked around and made out his bulky shape under the blankets of the bed, little grunting snores accompanying his slow, heavy breathing. One of his hands dangled down the bedside from under its covers.

Aimee carefully walked across the room, avoiding the whisky bottle and empty beer cans, and gently took hold of the hand. Its warmth and sweatiness made her shiver but then a thought struck her and she whispered to him, "I hope you're wearing something... Take me to the garden of Scowcroft House please."

He was wearing something, just. The grubby grey underpants were not very fetching but at least they spared Aimee's blushes. Walmsley couldn't care less what he looked like; he was still sleeping off the beer and whisky as he lay on the grass in the sun.

Although she giggled as she asked the bottle to take her home, Aimee was very relieved to be away from him and into the last stages of their plans. She got back to the house just as the glazier began knocking at the front door. Remembering about him she ran down stairs and let him in just as Mum's car pulled up in the driveway and as Jamie was dragged into the garden by Cuddles.

"Well here we are, the whole smashing family home at once!" the glazier quipped, "Any more accidents for me to look at or is it just the bedroom window this time?"

"Just the window I hope," Mum said sternly, "You know where it is I presume… you two, in the kitchen now… we've got a little problem to solve!"

They hurried into the kitchen and, after Jamie had given Cuddles his dinner and Aimee had put the kettle on, they sat down around the table.

"I've had a phone call from the British Embassy in Italy, they've found Mike in a hospital and it seems he's been there in a coma for the past two years. They are going to put him on a flight back to Britain this afternoon, but I'd like to know how he managed to be here last week if he was in a coma. I think that you two owe me a bit of an explanation don't you?"

"Yes, Mum… but we can't tell you everything just yet, not until Dad is back with us and Walmsley and Lough are locked away. It's all part of our big plan you see and we promised Dad we wouldn't say anything until gets here as well. But he has been in hospital in a coma like the Embassy said, only when he woke up he managed to get away and make his way back here without the hospital knowing. He must have been able to get back in again when he went back there and now they've found him again. He'll have to tell you how he did it, Mum and I think you should act all innocent and back him up with the Embassy, and don't let on he's been back here." Aimee warned.

"Well that won't be hard seeing as how I know nothing anyway! And the other thing is that the police rang me back about Lough, they found him on the doorstep and took him back to the police station. It seems they were looking for him in connection with a murder so we were right to ring about him."

"Great!" Jamie exclaimed, "One down, one to go!"

"Er… Mum, you don't have some money spare do you… about two hundred pounds… to pay the Glassman," Aimee asked, remembering that she still hadn't found a way of getting the money herself. "I was supposed to get it as a reward for finding Cuddles only they decided they didn't want him back so I can't pay for the window."

"Two hundred pounds! Well I certainly haven't got that sort of money. He'll have to wait for it, tell him to send us a bill. He won't mind, after all we are his best customers. Oh, I forgot to tell you, I rang to report the telephone so expect someone round to fix that as well… And we're not paying them yet either!"

When they'd had had their sardine salad and cups of tea, Mum got herself ready and went off back to work. The glazier came down the stairs soon afterwards and grumbled about not being paid but accepted it as he couldn't deny that they were good customers. And as Aimee opened the door to let him leave another man was standing on the doorstep ready to repair the telephone wires.

"Watch out for this lot mate, they're a right set of rogues," the glazier told him with a weary shake of his head as he walked towards his van.

The telephone man looked at Aimee who merely shrugged her shoulders, pointed out the cut wires and added, "A murderer did it, ask the police to pay you … they've got him now."

Chapter 17

Home

The early evening local news on television was full of the arrest of James Lough for the murder of Mr. William Mackie and the next morning the local radio was taken over by reports of a massive diamond, drug and people smuggling operation being smashed. There was another frantic burst of news the next day when it was rumoured that the ring leader was a prominent local businessman who had been caught red handed (and red faced, Aimee quipped as she told Jamie about Walmsley's underpants) at the docks supervising the unloading of the latest shipment. The police had then driven the van to its next rendezvous and managed to arrest some very big names in the criminal world in London.

To put the finishing touches to a brilliant weekend Dad was delivered home, much to his delight, by two very pretty ladies, WPC Julie Williams and WPC Sharon Mc.Naughton. His smiles did not last too long however as Mum whisked him off to the kitchen, slammed the door shut behind her and had a lengthy discussion about hospitals and Italy and honesty. When he came out again, opening the door so quickly that Aimee and Jamie nearly fell into the kitchen; he looked ready for another stay in hospital.

The final two bricks in the happiness wall were put into place first by a phone call telling Mum that she was to receive a one thousand pound reward for helping to capture Lough. The second was her decision to order a Chinese banquet for four from the 'Golden Pagoda.' Cuddles was given an extra helping of, 'Meaty Mouthfuls' for his part in the proceedings!

It was a few weeks later when the Dancing Sally had been returned to Dad's ownership that Aimee finally told Jamie what she was going to do with Larus. He'd never guessed where she had put the sphere and she took great delight in showing him.

"Oh I knew it was there but I didn't want to disappoint you by saying I knew," he fibbed despite his blushes telling the truth.

Dad managed to get a bank loan to get the Sally re-fitted and a new crew was sorted out - mostly made up of his old crew with the addition of Daniel Mackie, Billy's son. The day before she was due to go out on her first trip, Aimee managed to persuade Dad to take her, Mum and Jamie for a special trip with a picnic on board. Daniel came along too to help man the boat and get to know her. Cuddles was left at home sleeping off a long morning walk on the beach; making gulls scatter and digging in the sand for something really smelly.

The sky was cloudless and the sea mirror-calm when, a couple of hours out from port, Dad dropped anchor and they all tucked in to Mum's specially prepared feast. When all the sandwiches had been eaten and the last chocolate éclair had been sucked empty of cream and devoured, Dad settled down to an afternoon nap. Mum got out her knitting and her crossword book and managed to do both at once. Jamie and Daniel got out their fishing rods and soon had their lines over the side and were swapping stories about Billy. As for Aimee, she had invited along one more passenger; one wrapped in an old carrier bag.

She made her way to the stern of the boat and with some relief she whispered, "Good riddance to bad rubbish!" as she let Walmsley's gun and the Star Fall sphere drop out of the bag to disappear with hardly a splash and sink swiftly down to the cold darkness of the seabed.

"Can anyone help me with this one?" Mum suddenly called out, "It's got eight letters and the clue is… 'Flowers of the month for this tree,' whatever that means."

Aimee and Jamie looked at each other across the deck. The same memory enveloped both of their minds; Thomas May in his cottage saying, "Aimee and Jamie, such a lovely rhyme and Hawthorn, how apt that you should bear that name."

213

But before they could give Mum the answer that they had both worked out, Dad opened one eye and called out, "May blossoms on the Hawthorn tree… I bet even Aimee and Jamie knew that!"